Other Titles by *Langaa* RPCIG

The Woman Who Ate Python & Other Stories

Sammy Oke Akombi

Langaa **Research & Publishing CIG**
Mankon, Bamenda

Publisher:
Langaa RPCIG
(*Langaa* Research & Publishing Common Initiative Group)
P.O. Box 902 Mankon
Bamenda
North West Province
Cameroon
Langaagrp@gmail.com
www.langaapublisher.com

ISBN:9956-558-01-x

DISCLAIMER
All views expressed in this publication are those of the author and do not necessarily reflect the views of Langaa RPCIG.

Content

1

The Woman Who Ate Python

In the fullness of day, whenever the impulsive clouds decide to disperse, the rays of the sun settle radiantly on the immense form of the Cameroon mountain and expose its striking majesty to every eye that stops to face it. The slope is gentle that slants to the left and the same for the other that slants to the right. At the foot of the left slope lies Bonakunda village, a community of about one hundred households living their own life as it had been divinely handed down to them.

The men of this community had so much respect for their women folk that they regarded them like jewellers do precious stones. Or even better, like pearl divers treat their finds. This explains why some of them who had an overflowing tendency of acquisition, tended to work extra hard in order to acquire as many women as possible. Palaces in nearby "fondoms" prided on enormous collections. The "fons" and other notables of these "fondoms" knew better than anyone else that without women the continuity of a lineage could be everything but assured.

The Bonakunda woman was therefore treated with utmost care, in fact like the stigmas of a sweet smelling flower. They were restricted from any adventure, the community considered to be dangerous to their health and well-being. They did not have to hold a machete for the purpose of clearing virgin forest nor cutting anything hard. They should only handle hoes to prepare the soft soil for planting. They did not have to climb coconut trees to harvest their nuts nor climb palm trees to cut down their cones nor tap them for their sweet wine. Although the women used firewood for cooking, only men had to cut and split the wood for them. They had no right to expose their voluptuous bodies as they went about their daily businesses in the village. In this way, they avoided setting on the fire in the sex vultures of the community. So they did not only dress decently but they also spoke discreetly and led their lives in both discretion and decency. No wonder, the Bonakunda community, for its nearly two centuries of existence was yet to register a single case of rape. In fact, rape was an alien concept which the typical Bonakundan was yet to contemplate. Also, in order to sustain the woman's disciplined disposition, the community had imposed certain gastronomic restrictions. For instance, the Bonakunda woman must not eat the meat of a python. It was believed that if she did it, the children she would bear after that would live to crawl on their bellies.

In this regard, a woman could cook python for men to eat without tasting of it, not even the accompanying sauce. For generation after generation, no woman in Bonakunda had questioned the belief. They all felt that it was in their interest that such beliefs existed. A woman grew up in the community with a proper understanding of her role. Her dream as a girl was to grow up, get married and assume her natural function: to willingly conceive, give birth and nurture babies for her own good, the good of her family and that of the entire community. When she got married, she was all respect for her husband, the prospective father of her children. She called him my lord and answered him in like manner. She knew she did not have to disobey him. At least not publicly. She understood perfectly well that her lord her husband was her only one and able man.

One blessed day, a very beautiful baby was born in the Esunge family of Bonakunda. Her birth was rather unusual. She had embraced the world feet first instead of head first. It was quite difficult for her mother whose name was Ndolo. However, she arrived safely and was called Ebenye. She grew up like other children in the community, imbibing the values and upholding them. At two, her mother expected to have a younger sister or brother for her but that did not happen. By the time she had turned six, Ndolo knew Ebenye was and would remain her only child. She was going to spoil her, but Mola Esunge had other wives who understandably were Ebenye's mothers. They had children, some of whom were about Ebenye's age. She was naturally attracted to these half sisters and brothers. This helped her a lot as it made her escape the spoiling tendencies of her mother. However, there was something strange about her. She was unusually talkative and inquisitive, sometimes, much to the embarrassment of her mothers and father. One afternoon, after Mola had called for her to bring him some water to

3

drink, she decided she would find out a few things that had not been quite straight in her mind.

"Mola, is there anything wrong with having only one mother?" she asked.

"There's nothing wrong with that Ebenye", her father answered.

"Nothing wrong father?" she insisted.

"No, nothing wrong my daughter", her father assured her.

"Then what am I doing with one, two, three, four, five mothers?" she asked still counting her fingers.

"What you are doing with five mothers? But that is a good thing for you my child. If I hadn't the money to marry them, you would have had only one mother," Mola said feeling satisfied.

"It's good not to have money then", Ebenye remarked.

"Why?" asked Mola, a little confused.

"Because when there's no money, a child will have only one mother and they will pay attention to each other, know each other better and help one another always."

"Come on Ebenye, you are only a child, there's much you still have to learn. Had I not married your other mothers, would you have had brothers and sisters?" Mola asked.

"No, Mola but Ndolo is usually by herself whenever I go to help my other mothers. They call me and send me to carry out one errand or another or do one chore or another. And you know, when I'm not with Ndolo, nobody else is," Ebenye complained.

"Well, it is her fault. She must not keep away from your other mothers. And your fault too Ebenye. You always go to meet your brothers and sisters in your other mothers' homesteads. You never ask them to come over to Ndolo's . Try to take them there. She's their mother too. They must go there and play for as long as they're free. So from today, take all your brothers and sisters to Ndolo's homestead, you understand me?" Mola said instructively.

"All right, Mola, I don't know why I have not been able to think of it all this time," she said and went off to another part of the compound.

The following evening, Ebenye brought four of her half brothers and six of her half sisters to Ndolo's hut. Although they all lived in the same compound, Ndolo had never been honoured with the presence of such a crowd in her hut before. She welcomed them and they all sat around the fire and told folk tales. The children took turns in telling stories and she listened with keen interest. When they had finished, Ndolo brought out a white bowl full of dark plums. She handed three to each of the children. They roasted them in the fire and ate. Then she cleared her throat and said, "My dear children I have been very happy listening to your interesting stories. I also think I should tell you one myself. Are you ready to listen?"

"Yes we are," they chorused.

"What is your story about?" they chorused again.

"My story" she said, "is about a naughty girl who kept turning down suitors."

"A long time ago, in this our self-same village,' she began, "it was difficult for a girl to refuse a suitor. Once parents had found a suitor for their ripe daughter she had no right to refuse the man. She believed in her parents and she knew everything her parents did was in her interest. Nevertheless, a beautiful girl was born in the village. When she grew up to the age of sixteen, her beauty was so remarkable that people in other villages as far as Kokobuma heard about her. In fact, people simply called her Beauty. She became a hotly-sought-after bride not only because of her beauty but because she was also found to be strong and hardworking. One by one, men came to marry her but each time her parents presented a man to her, she turned him down. It was the first time such a thing had happened but Beauty's parents were patient and very understanding. More men came but non of them made an impression on Beauty. Her mother became very worried and had to talk to her one day. "My daughter, it appears, if men were made by carpenters, you would have given them specifications to make the type of man you want for a husband."

"Mama," Beauty said "I won't go as far as that but I can assure you that when the one I would willingly address 'My Lord and only one" comes by, I will readily accept him. All it takes is time and patience." And patience she really had, for she kept turning down suitors for the following ten years. One day, a young man of about thirty years old showed up in the village. He was about two metres tall. He had an oval face, adorned with a glossy moustache. His chocolate-coloured skin shone with a brilliance that could be compared only to a piece of polished ivory in the sun. Above all, his face wore such charm that could disarm even the queen of frigidity. His smile struck Beauty, who was then twenty-six, an excruciating blow. Nobody could tell if she ever recovered from the effect of this blow. People in the village found it difficult to call this man any other name than Mr. Fineboy.

When Mr. Fineboy first arrived in the village, he went straight to see Beauty's parents. They were already fed up taking suitor after suitor to their daughter, so they asked him to present himself to her directly. He did and the blow that had already struck her fell again and it was shattering. The marriage was quickly contracted without anyone bothering to find out where the young man had come from. The following day, Mr. Fineboy took his bride away to nobody-knew-where. The couple did not even bother to take along an escort. Only the two of them started their journey. It was on horseback. After several kilometres, they arrived in a village where the young man handed the horse over to somebody and they continued the journey on foot. Beauty complained but Mr. Fineboy simply asked her not to worry. After walking for about twenty kilometres, they arrived at another village where Fineboy again handed in all his clothes. Beauty again complained but he said he had better clothes in the next village. On getting to it several hours after, he handed in his legs and continued the journey somersaulting. By then

Beauty's shock was too much for her. It was as if she was going through a nightmare. She thought of escaping, but she did not even know where she was. It was really amusing and at the same time frightening to see her Fineboy somersaulting as they journeyed on. "Single-handedly I have brought myself to this" she thought regrettably as she kept on consuming kilometre after kilometre on foot with a somersaulting husband at her side.

When they arrived at the next village, he handed in even those arms he used for his somersaults and started rolling on the ground. Beauty had become quite used to the whole spectacle and was only expecting the worst. And in fact, the worst came when he handed in the trunk and was left only with his head. The movements of the head was like that of a frog, leaping from spot to spot. Beauty could not exactly stand it. She attempted to run away but she started feeling hard blows around her body. Many more bodiless heads had surrounded her. They were leaping and landing on her. When she turned around and saw many more leaping toward her, she fainted. She lay unconscious for about two hours. When she regained consciousness, she noticed her bodiless husband and the entire family-in-laws around her. She immediately understood her plight and thought aloud.

Oh what will my poor mother and father think.
Finding out my choice of a man had turned out to be a thing so, so abhorrent.
Oh what a sting to live amongst
Creatures, things that stink.

8

After she had said this, she fainted again and this time it was for good. Till this day, neither her parents nor any other person in the village knew what had happened to her.

My dear children, any community in which you are born remains your community and it is your shepherd. Like every committed shepherd, its every move is in the best interest of the sheep he shepherds. But as you are not sheep, question what your shepherd does but do not treat him like a floor rag. Well children," she concluded "it is already late now. Go to bed everyone and sleep well. I promise you some more stories tomorrow."

Days were constant as they ran into months and finally months into years. The years handed out maturity to every living thing including Ebenye. It was her turn, and that of other girls of her age, to get married. Her mother was worried about her because she was naturally tomboyish and rather outspoken. She felt she had done her best to make her inculcate the values of the Bonakunda people, but she still feared she might disappoint her. She counted on her for as many grand children as possible, since she had not had many children herself. She became really expectant when her daughter attained a marriageable age.

A man called Ekinde was the first to show any interest in Ebenye. Most of the other marriageable men were scared of her. "That tiger of a woman," they would often remark, "will tear any man apart before he realizes it." Nevertheless,

Ekinde approached the family and made his intentions known. Ndolo was very much relieved and she felt very happy. Ekinde was not only young but he was also a hunter. Hunters were said to make the best sons-in-laws. And Ekinde had only recently been given the best hunter award by the chief of Bonakunda. Ndolo called her daughter beforehand and meticulously explained the situation to her. She even reminded her of the story of Beauty which she had told them several years before. Ebenye was very touched by her mother's concern. So at the age of 22, Ebenye got married to Ekinde who was ten years older. Since then the couple had lived through the rugged path of marriage, where the rough patches were usually more visible than the smooth.

There was this day, Ekinde had just returned from one of his hunting trips. He threw down the hunting bag that he had been carrying on his back and sat down in the kitchen, feeling very tired. Ebenye came in and immediately genuflected saying "Welcome my lord."

"Thank you my lovely one," he answered. She looked at the bulging bag. It seemed to her, it was full of game. She immediately turned over the contents. It was a large python that covered the floor. Fortunately it was dead but she could not restrain the urge to let out a shout, so she did.

"Would you keep quiet," Ekinde growled, "who sent you to the bag anyway?" She however, summoned courage and looked at the dead snake sprawled on the floor. It measured about six metres long, and fifty centimetres in diameter. In the tradition of the Bonakunda people, python is royal meat and it must be eaten only in the palace by distinguished elders of the community – all of them men of course.

As soon as Ekinde had had his bath he sat down and had his supper. Immediately after supper, he went to the palace to inform the chief about the python. The chief sent one of his advisers to go with Ekinde and evaluate the snake. After the adviser had reported back, the chief assigned four men including Ekinde to have it butchered. Three women including Ebenye were assigned to do the cooking. She was the leader of the group. The meal must be ready the next day.

It was evening, and a cool one at that. It had drizzled in the afternoon. All the men who mattered in Bonakunda were seated in the palace with their appetites sharpened for the special meal. Ebenye was motioned to bring it in. Two giant pots were put in front of the chief, one containing the meat and sauce while the other contained specially boiled plantains. The chief sat facing all the distinguished elders who were in horseshoe formation. Immediately Ebenye and the two other women had finished placing the pots, they were asked to return to their homesteads. One of the elders was delegated to ensure the sharing of the food. He in turn requested a young man to open the pots and spread out some whittled plantain leaves on the floor. On the leaves he asked the young man to place the meat piece by piece. As he did so the elder examined the pieces carefully. Some of them were special and meant to be eaten by the chief only. One of such pieces was the chest of the snake. He turned the pieces over and over and could not find this particular piece. He raised his head and announced to the people sitting that a piece of the python was missing. Everybody was surprised. Such a thing had never happened before and so they wondered why it should happen this time. They called on the hunter to explain but he too only showed surprise. He told them that when he and the other three people who had been assigned to butcher the python were doing the job, every piece was intact, including the chest of the snake. After Ekinde had explained this, someone suggested that the women who had cooked the python be summoned. Some of the elders found it unnecessary, considering that women never tasted python. They did not imagine that a woman could be responsible for the missing piece of meat. Others however said that they should still be summoned having prepared the meal. At least, they would say whether they had seen the missing part or not. Finally, they decided to summon Ebenye, their leader. When she entered, one of the distinguished elders declared in a solemn tone:

"Our dear and respectable wife, would be mother of our children, we have no doubt that you understand our customs very well. We also trust, you know that we expect to find every single piece of the python you have cooked for us. But we have found to our consternation that a piece of the python, the chest has disappeared. Do you have anything to tell us?"

"I've heard what you've said my lord" replied Ebenye, "but you all know that I'm only a woman, who is not allowed to even taste of the sauce of the meat I've cooked for you. How can I then muster the courage to take a piece of the meat?" she queried.

"Well, we don't imagine that you can do such a thing," another elder said, "but we just wanted to make sure that you had nothing to do with the disappeared piece of python. By the way, in the course of cooking, did you, by any chance, see the said piece?"

"Yes, I did" she answered.

Ekinde and the other butchers nodded approvingly.

"Well, my lords, "Ebenye said, "can I go now?"

"Yes, you can go," they chorused.

Ebenye turned towards the door and moved one, two, three steps and then stopped. She turned around and faced the men brazenly. She started talking to them, "My lords, I'm not sure for how long you'll continue to treat us like some precious property of yours. The way you treat our mothers and us their female children is as if we are simply instruments of your amiable pleasure. Some sort of pearl that is exhibited to show other people, how wealthy you are and after such exhibition it is tugged away until another occasion arises," she continued.

By now everyone sitting was quiet. Quiet not because they did not feel like speaking but they were simply stunned. Ebenye had taken all of them aback. They were waiting for what would come next. She cleared her throat and continued "I couldn't imagine how I would continue to serve people, as a matter of fact, cook for people and not have the pleasure of tasting what I've cooked. Naturally, I don't like eating snakes but I had to eat the chest of that Python. I ate it and it is lodged right here in my stomach." The so-called repercussions I'm waiting for anxiously. Let me give birth to kids that will crawl on their bellies. I think, I personally have had enough of this meanness!" she ended stamping her right foot on the floor.

For a good sixty-seconds, the room remained silent. None of the men could find his voice. Not even Ekinde. Shortly after, an elder found his voice. He coughed slightly and asked quietly. "Do you really mean to tell us that you, a woman, ate the chest of a Python?"

"Yes I did" Ebenye replied firmly and seditiously.

"Can you eat another piece of the Python, so that we all can be living, and authentic witnesses of a Python eating woman?" he requested.

"Yes of course," she said and moved to the pot that was still standing open.

She picked up a piece of Python, tore it in smaller pieces and ate them one by one. The men sat in absolute confusion as they watched the action. To them it was like a bad dream. No one imagined it was real. It was like watching someone drinking the bile of a python. Even Ekinde could not believe that it was his own wife that was creating and recreating the drama they were watching. He felt like stone. He could not get himself up. As Ebenye continued with the drama, Ekinde gradually recovered. He got up and like a lion he roared at his wife, "have you gone out of your mind? Eh Ebenye? What's gone into you woman?"

Without waiting to get an answer he lurched towards her and swung his right arm. Ebenye ducked and Ekinde lost balance and found himself staggering to the ground. But before he got down completely Ebenye stooped and picked him up like a hawk would do an unguarded chick. In one startling movement Ekinde was wriggling on the left shoulder of his wife. The whole assembly was dumbfounded as they watched the award-winning hunter desperately wriggling on the shoulder of a woman. Suddenly Ebenye held Ekinde gently and placed him buttocks-down on the floor. Everyone thought Ekinde would get up and walk out in shame but far from it he roared like a hungry lion that had just missed its prey and then rushed at Ebenye like an elephant which had just got a bullet between its eyes. Just then the chief found his voice and called out firmly "Ekinde! Ekinde! Stop! Stop it."

He stopped and turned to the chief. He was breathing like a hunter who had just dropped from the claws of a dying lion. With much pity the chief looked at him and said, "Ekinde, do not raise another finger against your wife. What she has just demonstrated shocks all of us. The whole experience has been especially traumatising for

15

me but thanks to the spirits of our ancestors, I have been able to keep my wits together. What this woman, your wife, our daughter has done", he said pointing to Ebenye," is very, very important for our community. If the event hasn't revealed anything to you, I think it has to me. It has opened my eyes wide to see what our forefathers had refused to see, generation after generation. I know no-one can have the courage to eat the meal we all had gathered here for, so you can all return to your homes and my dear people, all that we of Bonakunda can do in the present circumstances is to open our minds and wait and see if the children this brave woman, Ebenye bears will live to crawl on their bellies."

2

Death of the Dead Man

Nkwomen rose from a gutter just as the sun was getting on its marks. He belched, yawned, and then through his anus, he noisily released some gas that had been fighting its way out of his bowels. This adulterated the freshness of the morning air. His surroundings immediately acquired the putrid pungency of a decaying carcass, which did not bother him at all. Instead he chuckled, then gargled and cleared his throat, releasing a loud cough which rattled his chest and even his rib bones. He spat the mucus on his left palm and then examined it with the shrewdness of a medical laboratory analyst. He saw some crimson stains on it. Gently, he wiped the mucus off his hand, on no where else but the pair of baggy trousers he was wearing. Later, he took off his jacket, examined it meticulously and put it on again. He heaved a sigh and asked himself a question which the people of Saloko had come to identify him with:

"Abeh yi eh?"

Without expecting an answer from anyone, he gave the response himself:

"Abveh mbakenem Ooo!"

Again he sighed, walked a short distance and repeated the same question, this time in Pidgin English:

"Wuskayn pikin she born eh?"

He did not hesitate to provide the answer himself:

"she born na man pikin Ooo!"

As he was about to make his way home, he realised that he had pains all over his body. Besides, a feeling of nausea had started pestering him. He looked around and found the trunk of a long dead tree lying invitingly at the road side. He walked to it and slumped on it. He lowered his head and gave vent to smelly swill that came out through his mouth. When the swill stopped flowing out, he felt some relief. He then placed his head in his cupped palms and turned unusually pensive.

He thought about his past and imagined the mood in which his mother might have been on that glorious day – the day of his birth. How she might have felt very relieved after an obviously turbulent experience of parturition. And when his father had learnt that the baby, his own baby had been born and was a male, he might have jumped for joy and performed some agile and waist-twisting movement that could have easily spelt him out as an unequalled dancer of 'enook', 'bikutsi" or "mapuka".

"Yes," Nkwomen continued thinking, "everybody in Saloko, might have been happy, really happy that a male had been born, the more cherished of babies, the more sought after. Carefully, he thought about his present, then his past, and attempted contemplating the future, which he could not exactly figure out. It was rather very confusing. Finally, he shook his head, took it out of his cupped palms, looked blankly at

18

the far away horizon and concluded that he was likely an epitome of a wasted generation.

The sun rays were getting warmer and warmer when he got up from the tree trunk. He rubbed some dirt off his trousers and slowly walked home. On his way, both men and women hailed him as he passed by.

"Nkwomen neyi eh!" they would greet.

"Ooo ma" or "Ooo ta," he responded, depending on whether the response was directed to a woman or a man. As he went along, tongues wagged, making both sympathetic and derisive comments, like on the occasion where, a man after observing Nkwomen walk past, clapped his hands in desperation and exclaimed: waow, the womb can produce oo!"

"Produce eh-what?" asked a woman who was standing by him.

"Look at that ... eh ... what can I call it? Is a product of the womb eh", said the man mischievously.

"So you think it's only the womb to blame for the production of people like that in this community. What about the loins of a man?" questioned the woman.

Do you mean to say that he came out of man's loins?" asked the man.

"Not exactly but the loins caused it into the womb," replied the woman.

"My sister" said the man, "causing something into a womb doesn't compel that womb to produce it."

"In the same way, producing something does not always compel the producer to ensure its

19

safety. I agree that the womb produced that drunkard of a Nkwomen, but ever since the womb released him, where has he lived? Obviously not in another womb, I suppose," the woman said with much conviction.

"I've got your message," said the man. "You mean to say that we all in Saloko are in fact the culprit."

While the people were fidgeting, gossiping and bothering about him, Nkwomen went his way, undeterred. Before he eventually opened the door, into the safety of his room, he passed by a public tap, where many children were struggling to fetch water for their various homes. As soon as they saw him, their struggles stopped momentarily and they chorused:

"Dead man! Dead man!" He simply waved back raising his right shoulder a few centimetres higher than usual. When he finally faced his door, he put his hand in the right pocket of his baggy trousers and took out his key. He put it into the padlock, turned it twice and it gave way. The hinges welcomed him with a slight tinkle, letting the four walls of the room open up to a wam embrace. His bed appeared to have heaved a sigh of relief as it anticipated an immediate end to the abandonment of the previous night. He sat on it, feeling really tired. He pulled off his boots, yawned loudly and asked himself once again:

"Abveh yi eh?"
Shortly after, he responded:
"Abveh mbakanem oo."

Then, he stretched out on the bed, closed his eyes and succumbed to the salutory benevolence of deep sleep. Even though Nkwomen had become one of the scum of Saloko, it was not entirely his fault. He had been a rare bird in his primary school days. He had in fact been a village celebrity. He was loved by everyone in the village, especially because he used to exhibit much ingenuity in everything he did. He was easily the best in every school subject and activity. He captained the school athletic, and football teams that had won all the zonal trophies for primary school competitions. It was no surprise in Saloko when he came out top in all the public examinations, he had sat for. He was however unfortunate that he had grown up without the warmth and care of a mother. She had passed away when he was only four. He lived an ill-favoured life with his father who was not able to take another wife. He was a very skilful weaver of mats. He did not own a farm, so he depended solely on his mat weaving. After weaving a few of them, he would take them to the local market and sell. He would use some of the money to buy food and the rest would be frittered away on palm wine. He drank like a fish and was lucky that like a fish, he was never drunk. He could all by himself, drink a jug of palm wine and still ask for more in a very sober tone. Because he drank a lot, it was quite understandable that he took up palm wine tapping, as a secondary occupation. He would collect a jar of palm wine from a tapping session, take it to the market, sell it and use the money to buy palm wine and drink with friends. If anybody asked him why he sold palm wine to buy palm wine, he would hit his chest and say arrogantly: "you see, variety is the spice of life. Variety, I tell you, is the spice of life." At this point he would turn around and ask his audience if they did not agree with him. And sure they always did.

So, tomorrow was not an issue, as far as Nkwomen's father was concerned. He was one of such people who believed that tomorrow always had a way of taking care of itself. In this regard, he had adopted a *chop-broke-pot* attitude of life, ever since his wife died. No wonder, Nkwomen had started looking after himself at a very early age. He did little jobs in order to pay his fees at the primary school and also buy his books and uniforms. One of the public exams in which he was top was the entrance exam into government colleges. Naturally, he was offered a place in one of them. Some of the adults who wished him well had encouraged him and had made him write the examination. They had also tried, in vain, to prevail on his father to contribute in sending his son to secondary school. To everyone's surprise he complained that he had not even gone through primary education himself so he could not understand why his son should be so hot about secondary school. He thought a successful completion of primary education was good enough for a boy from a poor family. Secondary education was a luxury that only the children of the rich could afford. They alone could stay behind desks for all their lives, if they so wished. As for poor people's children, they must start earning a living as soon as they could. He even thought it would be dangerous for his son to improve on his education because he would not be able to inherit poverty which was the only inheritance he could oblige him with. Generation after generation of members of his family had been known to bequeath only poverty to their posterity, so he thought it would be unfair if he went out of his way to bequeath his son everything but poverty. He concluded that education usually engendered riches and power, and he was in no mood to take the risk of offending his ancestors. Nkwomen's sympathisers however insisted that the boy had got a scholarship award and he would require just a little financial assistance from his parents. Whatever that meant, had not gone down well with him. However, he asked them to do whatever they liked with his son but he had warned that he would not welcome anybody who might come back to him requesting him to assist a son who might have been sent out of school for whatever reason. The group of well-wishers were, however, not discouraged. They contributed generously to raise some money for Nkwomen's registration fees and the buying of his school requirements.

The registration fee was handed to him on a bright Monday morning and as soon as it got into his hands, his entire body started screaming happiness. He rushed to the bathroom and had his bath, and a few minutes later, he was getting ready to go to the grammar school campus. He did his best to be tidily dressed. Assured that he still had a full day before registration was closed, he walked hopefully to the premises of the grammar school, situated ten kilometres from Saloko. On arrival, he could not cope with the rivulets of sweat that ran down his face and body. He went into one of the bathrooms and cleaned himself up as neatly as possible. He then studied himself in a mirror to make sure he was presentable enough to meet the principal. Satisfied, he went looking for the office. He was shown into the secretariat where the secretary rudely told him, the principal was too busy to receive anyone. He pleaded that his case was urgent and the secretary insisted on having an idea about what he wanted to meet the principal for. He told her and she said that it was not necessary to see the principal, for it was too late. He thought she was joking, because according to him the deadline for registration was yet to expire. She however turned the knob of the door that led into the principal's office and when it opened, he forced himself into it. It was a large cosy room whose calmness and serenity was only disturbed by a light humming of the air-conditioner which stayed stuck on the opposite wall. On the large mahogany table, behind which sat an ebony-black-man with round cheeks that glittered with a healthy sheen, were files, a telephone receiver, some fat books and a gold plaque on which shone the inscription:

Mr Tekena Hayaki, B.Sc. (Hons). CAPES.
PROVISEUR

As he walked in gently, the seemingly busy principal raised his balding head and asked:

"What's your problem young man?"

"I've come to pay my registration fee and secure my place, sir," said Nkwomen.

"That isn't paid to me, is it?" the principal asked.

"I don't know sir," said the boy.

The principal was surprised at the answer, and he looked at the boy carefully and then asked:

"Who are you by the way?"

"I'm Nkwomen sir. Nkwomen Taloko from Saloko sir," said the boy uneasily.

"You wish to secure a place in class…"

"Class one sir, form one."

That's all right," said the principal. "You'll need to see the *intendant*."

"*Intendant*. What's that sir?" asked the boy looking confused.

The principal was again surprised, but he soon checked himself and said:

"I'm sorry, I mean the bursar. Pay your registration fee to the bursar, ok. My secretary will tell you where to find him."

"Yes sir, thank you sir," Nkwomen said hopefully.

At the bursar's a list was consulted but Nkwomen's name was not found on it. So, his registration fee was not accepted. Instantly, anxiety took over the better part of him and sweat started finding its way again through the pores of his skin. He went back to the principal and informed him that his name had not been found on the bursar's list. He checked his own list and observed that Nkwomen's name was on it and as a matter of fact he had one of the highest scores. He picked up his phone and dialled the bursar's number. At the end of the conversation, he dialled the vice principal's and also had a talk with him. He put down the phone and turned to Nkwomen saying:

"I'm sorry, your place has been taken up."

"Who by? If I may ask sir," enquired Nkwomen.

"By someone else on the waiting list," answered the principal.

"But sir, for all I know, registration closes today and that will be at the end of the day" said Nkwomen almost in tears.

"Well boy, for all I know too, registration closed today and that was at the end of the last hour. Since you hadn't shown up all this time, the vice principal who is responsible for admissions, has had your name replaced by that of a more willing candidate."

"Isn't there anything you can do for me sir?" asked the boy desperately.

"Nothing my boy, nothing. It's too late. But wait a minute, how … eh … did you come?" asked the principal.

"I came on foot sir," answered the boy.

"All by yourself?"

"All by myself sir."

"Why? Haven't you got parents?"

"Not exactly sir."

"How is that?"

"My mother had died long ago and my father is not a willing parent," the boy explained tearfully.

"I see, but there's nothing we can do for you. The class is already full and we must comply with the government directive, which allows for only fifty students in a class. We can't possibly exceed that number my lad. If there was anything I could do, I would readily do it my boy, especially because you look quite promising. It might please you to know that you were even one of the best candidates in the entrance examination. Kids like you need to be encouraged. Try next time and good luck," the principal ended dismissively.

Nkwomen walked out of the office feeling very dizzy. The words: "The vice principal … has had to replace you with a more willing candidate" battered his mind like a hammer in the firm grip of a crazy carpenter. He shook his head mournfully to himself:

"How else could I have been more willing? Oh wretchedness! I think right now, I'm as good as dead. Surely I'm dead, a dead man!"

Back in Saloko, he gave back the money that had been given him for his registration and none of his well-wishers had the courage to follow up and reverse what had happened to him.

This was twenty years back but Nkwomen had since adopted the name Dead man. He had for the past twenty years led a life void of conviction, not giving a damn to whatever happened to him in the present nor in the future. He spent whatever money he had with so much ease and alacrity, deliberately adopting poverty as a faithful partner. He made his cherished alias very popular by always putting on a jacket he

27

picked up, at the "okrika line of business." It had
the inscription *"DEAD MAN"* boldy written on its
back. All the children in Saloko knew him by that
name. Whenever he was called, by it, he showed
so much high spirits that his walking steps got
close to those of the legendary *Charlie Chaplin* in
action. Moreover, he earned his living by working
for dead people. He had taken up this occupation
when his own father had died, fifteen years ago.
He had felt obliged to honour him by providing
him with an eternal resting place. Therefore
single-handedly, he dug up the grave in which his
father was buried. Since then a new career had
opened up for him - the Saloko area grave digger.
This occupation fetched him a lot of money,
because the frequency of death in Saloko had
recently doubled. A week hardly passed by
without a corpse in wait for burial. He was
always solicited. Even other villagers around
Saloko soon knew about him and they too began
sending for him, each time there was a death. His
business was actually enjoying a boom. A lot of
money in hand, with almost nothing to invest it
in, Dead man easily developed the potential that,
so far, had lain latent in him – a riotous rapacity
for alcohol. Palm wine was a ready and willing
prey and then as he grew richer, beer and spirits
registered as victims. He did not bother much
about food. He only took it to satisfy the yearning
of his stomach, he would dash to *Na man di loss*"
eating house, take a few mouthfuls of plantains
and beans, sometimes gari and okro soup or
simply pepper soup and then dash out again to
resume his drinking.

Nkwomen was an alcoholic but he never made himself a nuisance to the community. Whenever he drank above capacity, he would simply take off his famous jacket, sling it on his left shoulder and stagger home in peace. But when the capacity was far too high, he usually lay in a gutter and peacefully passed his night there disturbed only by crawling worms, mosquitoes, crickets and other creatures of the insect kingdom.

There was this day, Nkwomen was feeling rather tired. He had slept until the following morning, when he got up at cock-crow, although dawn had not fully dawned. He was on his bed, turning from side to side, feeling really bad. He also realised, there was a hollow in his stomach. He had pains all over his body and it seemed like he would never get out of bed. He had never felt that bad before, so he decided he would do something about it as soon as the day broke fully. When the sun timidly sipped in its first rays through the rafters of his unceiled room, he got up, not without difficulties, and managed to find his feet. They carried him laboriously to M'angaben's house. She owned and managed, "*Na man di loss*" eating house. Nkwomen asked for a plate of yams and hot pepper soup. He told her about his bad state and that he needed warm water for his bath. M'angaben knew Nkwomen's financial worth and so she did not hesitate to effect his order. Having eaten, Nkwomen went to the bathroom and had a satisfactory warm bath. He returned to his very willing bed, feeling that he would soon be all right. At nine o'clock that morning he knew it was not just hunger and fatigue that troubled him but something that required his going to the hospital. Before then, he had vowed never to step a foot of his in a hospital premises to seek treatment. After all, he had reckoned, he was already a dead man. Dead men had no use for medical care. He had thought that he would stay in his room and the pains and discomforts would go as gradually as they had come. When it dawned the following day, he could not wait to see the doctor. The night had been gruesome and things had not improved, rather they had grown worse. He consulted M'angaben once more and arrangements were made to take him to the hospital. There, he consulted a doctor and the diagnosis indicated that he was diabetic and he was also suffering from gout. He had to be admitted in the hospital for treatment to be effected for two months. This was a terrible period for him as he had no means to take alcohol. He was very lucky that M'angaben brought him two meals a day. Even when he was discharged from the hospital it was M'angaben who came to his assistance, lending him money to pay up the bills and to let his living take off once more.

On the day he was discharged, the doctor talked to him at length about the dangers of alcohol, especially when it was taken by a diabetic patient. After the homily, he was warned against further drinking of palm wine nor any other alcoholic drink. He considered this for a while and said to the doctor dejectedly: "But doctor, how can this be?" You see that I've been starved of alcohol, all these days that I've been under your charge. At this moment I feel like dying, just like someone who has been deprived of his life-blood. Desire for alcohol is a phenomenon that runs through the veins of our family tree. My own father, was an alcoholic, an admirable one, especially because he was a fish in the business. My grandfather too was no exception. You see nature is too strong to be abused by just anyone. I almost did it when I was young but where am I today? Really knee deep in it – a dead and dense alcoholic. Remember, he who tries to put on a fight against nature, is surely doomed to doom. As things are, I can't try such a thing doctor. I can't dare it doctor. I can't try not to be in the same business as my ancestors."

"Avoiding alcohol is to help preserve your health my dear friend," the doctor pursued. But if you insist on taking it then you are putting your life in great danger. In fact your death would be as sure as death itself."

"Good talk doctor," ripposted Nkwomen. The surer my death, the better for me. You know how children call me in the streets? – Dead man. Alcohol and alcohol alone is making me a living dead. Without it, I'm a dead Dead man with breath still pestering my lungs. And you know, a dead man that still retains his breath is worse off than a dead Dead man who has surrendered his. The latter is a complete dead man, unperturbed by existence be it drab or gay. So doctor, now that in your talk you have tied my ultimate end to alcohol, I'm really glad. I'll now drink and drink if only to hasten the ultimate end."

The doctor was absolutely embarrassed by Nkwomen's arguments. He wondered why he had come for treatment, in the first place. He knew he could do nothing to dissuade him and so he discharged him to his fate. He went home feeling strong and shortly after he resumed his grave-digging business, he easily made enough money to make good his indebtedness to M'angaben. His drinking took off in a gentle inclination but did not take long to grow steep. Each time anybody reminded him of the doctor's warning, he asked them if they knew the past tense of shit.

"How can the Dead man himself fear death," he would rant. "Was it not a learned man who said, he that was down needed fear no fall?" It's even my pleasure to come to grips with that death, whatever shape it might be. Death! Death! as if it has horns. I'm sure I wouldn't hate being at home with it anytime, anyhow, anywhere. After all, am I not Dead man myself?"

One day, Salako was not only ushered into dawn by the persistent crowing of the cocks but also by the eerie cries of the cats. The people soon realised that, nobody had done as much as catch a glimpse of the Dead man, the previous day. Even the children could not remember having had any occasion to give him the usual hailing. M'angaben too had only just realised that the Deadman had not shown up for his usual once-a-day meal. She became worried and went to his house to find out if he was all right. She knocked on his door softly. There did not seem to be any life within, yet the door had been bolted inside. She became alarmed, then she knocked desperately. Still no response, so she had to summon some other people. They came round and with the permission of the chief, they forced the door open. When they got in, each pair of eyes criss-crossed the other before settling on the figure on the bed. There lay Nkwomen, fully relaxed in the peace and ease of "sleep", his lips wearing a subtle smile. They all thought he was in a deep sleep. They tried to get him up but it was not the type of sleep that anyone could get up from.

News soon went round Saloko, about the death of the Dead man. All and sundry gathered around his doorsteps, waiting for their turns to give a stare at the corpse. Later, sympathisers— almost the entire community, spontaneously made generous contributions which were used to organise the funeral. A requiem mass was arranged, even though Dead man had hardly gone to church in his life time. A beautiful dark suit and a well-polished wooden coffin were bought for the Dead man's burial. His corpse was thoroughly cleaned and then clad in a resplendent manner. He even had a dark bow tie round his neck. The corpse was laid in state in front of his home. The whole community came out to pay their last respects to the Dead man. There was unexpectedly, so much fanfare at his funeral and even the heavens seemed to blaze when no-one had expected comets would be seen at his death. As he lay in state, waiting for the priest to perform funeral rites, the subtle smile that had embellished his face suddenly turned into a hostile frown.

3

I sat in the large auditorium, watching the endless ushering in of graduating students and their guests. We the young medical graduates had been lucky to be ushered in first. I sat down honourably on a seat that held the label bearing my name. I started wondering what the world would have in store for me after that day. I was going to take the Hippocratic Oath. As the wait prolonged, my inner self took pleasure in taking a walk down a long lane of distant memory.

Molrai is the name I grew up with, but I understand that when mother gave birth to me, father decided to call me Esong-Eri-Mmek. This name when translated from my mother tongue means "*the suffering on this earth.*" It did appear to my father that I was, from many indications, a symbol of the suffering on this earth. I have no reason to doubt him especially because generally, children are endowed with the fortune to grow up in the warmth, nurture and admonition of their parents, but I, on the contrary, have never known even the warm, sincere smile of a parent. I understand mama breathed her last the same minute I cried my first. What a way to embrace the earth! Papa could not wait to start calling me Esong-Eri-Mmek, after that. Twelve months later, on my first birthday, he too passed to the great beyond. My parental misfortune on this earth was therefore consummated, and on what day? My first birthday. The next name I heard people call me was Molrai, which stuck on me like a black stain on an immaculate surface, giving me a conspicuous identity. The name, in the language of my people means an orphan. Uncle Tuka-Tete, my papa's only brother, who had gone to settle in a foreign land called Kalushasha heard about the death and came home to pay his last respects to his lone brother.

After all the funeral rites had been performed and the accompanying celebrations had ended, Uncle had to return to Kalushasha. It was only natural that he took me along – his brother's only seed.

At the baby age of a little above one, I started my life at Uncle Tuka-Tete's house. He lived in a posh area of Lushasha, the capital city of Kalushasha. The area was called Mokolila. It had been carefully mapped out for people who mattered in the city. The parks, playgrounds, lawns and pavements had been fashioned by a really astute town planner. The houses spoke of architecture at-its-best. My uncle's villa stood imposingly in the middle of a well-kept garden that measured a little over a hectare. A solid fence surrounded the garden having an outlet only at the giant gate that stood enticingly at the side of the main road that led to adjoining villas. The grass lawns stayed eternally level like a mower's playground. The fruit trees and flowers were pruned to satisfy the taste of any aesthetic-conscious mind. The flora was complemented by a collection of fauna. This confirmed my uncle's taste for the good things of life. There were herds of rabbits and hares just for the pleasure of having them. There was a caged owl and other caged birds. A tamed parrot was part of the collection of birds. It had its liberty to move anywhere in the yard. A giant tortoise was also kept in the garden. Its habitat was a pit in which were pebbles and an artificial spring. Assorted fishes were also a great delight as they boisterously busied themselves in a well-kept pond. The villa had two floors – the ground and first floor. The ground floor housed the kitchen and a giant living room which was partitioned into three sections. Each section had a set of settees each structured in its own peculiar way to suit the class of guests who were received there. The most honoured guests were usually received in the plushest section. Two giant aquaria stood at each end of the living room. At one other corner stood a giant television set with a video deck attached. Every bedroom had its own set. A state-of-the-art "Akai" musical stereo set also stood by to spill out music just for the asking. So that if anyone was bored in this house then the one must be bored with life itself. On the first floor were the bedrooms and other accessories. Uncle was a polygamist, having all his three wives sheltered under the same roof. All three were materially satisfied but I could not tell if they were, emotionally and morally.

All the same, as far as I could observe, they all looked luxuriant and seemed to posses that verve which makes any man hit his chest and say, "what the hell have I done to wealth that it doesn't want to leave me alone?" They had twelve children among them and I was the thirteenth. We all grew up as one family of children, not easily identifying with a particular mother. Each of the three women was a mother to all of us and Uncle Tuka-Tete our most darling and respectable father. He rode a Limousine, a Mercedes 500. Our mothers all had cars that told the story of luxury, a BMW 728, a Jaguar and a Renault 25. There was a Pajero four-wheel drive that transported us, the children, to and from school and whenever we were obliged with an outing. I wondered whether any of us in the house at that time had the vaguest idea of the concept of poverty. We rarely got in contact with children from poor homes because the schools we attended were very expensive, where one met only with children whose parents or guardians were no less affluent than Uncle Tuka. The teachers themselves commanded a lot of respect because apart from their good training, there was none who came to work by public transport or on foot while their pupils were brought in or taken home in luxurious cars. They all had their own cars, good cars at that. The parties we attended could never have kept a poor soul at their ease. I lived under these ultra-pleasant conditions up to when I turned twelve.

I had just entered the first form of the secondary school, the most expensive in the city. It was called International Junior Cambridge. It had been created to discourage rich Kalushashans from sending their children abroad for primary and secondary education. Incidentally, studying in the school was not different from studying abroad in a so-called first world environment. The teachers were mostly foreigners, the school curriculum was virtually foreign. The students were being prepared for Cambridge examinations at the expense of local ones. We were young English students trained on African soil. I had hardly been through the first trimester when my fortunes suddenly went on reverse.

We, the ever-happy-boisterous-lot of the Tuka family, were all at dinner when Uncle entered with an unusual look masking his face. We all were surprised as the usual "hello dad" from each of us was only answered with a sad nod of the head. One of our mothers could not help but ask. It was Ngobu Osongo.

"Tete, you look rather funny. The dark cloud on your face is doing no good to our appetite. I wish you could clear it fast and oblige one with a smile.'

"It's no poetic matter Osongo, keep all that flowery language aside. It's a very serious matter. In fact I am in trouble. Blackmail, - that's the word. I've been blackmailed. An expulsion order is dangling over my head"

"Don't tell us that. What for? Is the General himself not your friend?" the utterances chorused spontaneously.

"Sure he is, but friends can sometimes decide to be unfriendly. Will you be surprised if I tell you that the same General is the originator of the blackmail?"

"I don't seem to understand you Tete but I think we had better suspend the topic. This is not the right time and place to discuss things like that. Come over and join us at table."

Uncle went into his room, minutes later he came down, pulled a chair and sat at table with the rest of us. He ate with utter indifference. His appetite must have run down several degrees. He barely pushed down the morsels that wobbly found their way into his mouth. After an equally reluctant drink, Ngobu Osongo, in company of the other two wives took uncle to his room.

"Now tell us dear, what exactly is amiss," the women asked in unison.

"Well, I have fallen out of favour with my friend the General and now he is threatening to expel me from this country."

"Expel you how? Are you an illegal alien? We suppose all your immigration papers are correct, and besides, we your wives are not only nationals of Kalushasha but also indigenes of three of the major tribes in the country. I in particular, am a full daughter of Lushasha. We shall give you all the required protection. Expelling our husband is tantamount to expelling us too. How then can anyone be expelled from their own country? Tete, it is our firm belief that nothing will happen to you. There's nothing to worry about."

"Woman you don't seem to know what you're talking about. How can you start a fight against the General, the all in all of this country? All power concentrates on, and radiates from him. How can you dare such a person in a fight. It's like putting up a fight against one's own creator."

"But can't the General change his mind?" the women chorused.

"Well he has his mind to himself, he can change it as he likes, but I'm afraid the present situation does not call for a change of mind. Just consider a flashback of his past and you will understand what I mean. He the General, with impunity expelled all fellow black people who used to live here under the pretext that they were illegal foreign immigrants. Well-meaning advisers tried in vain to prevail over him to see reason. They told him Africa was for all black people. It was only the white man in his scramble to satisfy his grab, grab tendency that gave it boundaries which of course are artificial. His ears were tone deaf to this argument and when the deadline matured, pregnant women, newly born kids, old and ailing fathers and mothers were strenuously evacuated across borders. He again with zeal spilt the blood of all who had preceded him in leadership for fear that they might harbour the temptation to taste power once again. He with vigour organised the crude murder of defenceless high court judges simply because they had resisted intimidation and failed to carry out his own side of what justice entailed. He shamelessly eliminated his own foreign minister, because he wanted to make the latter's beautiful wife his mistress. He told the entire world that a former Prime Minister that he himself had appointed was a foreigner simply because the latter had thought aloud of standing elections against him. You see, this is just a bird's-eye view of the past of him whom you think you can put up a fight against. I tell you women, ruthlessness, thy name is the General."

"We seem to understand now, how helpless our situation is, but Tete," pursued Ngobu Osongo, "how come that you have fallen out of favour with the General? Could you not have been tactful enough in your dealings with him?"

Uncle Tuka put down his head and seemed to have plunged into some communion with his inner self. When he took it up minutes later, it was to tell his anxiety weary audience:

"My wives, I must confess. I fell victim to incontinence, which is the bane of all of us humanity. I could not repress my desire for a woman, not any of you three, but another woman, one whom the General too could not close his eyes on. I was the winner which I always have been but the General could not take it gamely, rather he took it for a slight and has vowed to let me see red for daring that far. My wives, this vow is at the root of my impending troubles. I know him too well, my friend the General. He should by now be working on an order to expel me but it is so unexpected. All my investment is here. I don't even have as much as a hut in my own country. I'm in real soup – hot pepper soup. As a matter of fact, in a mess – reckless mess. O! Had I known ..."

"Had you known? But that's too late our dear dandy boy," Ngobu Osongo said provocatively.

"But my dear wives, you should at least forgive me. It's the weakness of the flesh. You know it, it fails one whenever there's a demand on it. You remember the most powerful man on

41

earth, even he too fell victim and put himself and his people to shame but at least his wife forgave him. I'll be very glad if you forgive me," Uncle Tuka pleaded.

"No way!" the wives chorused as Ngobu Osongo continued looking at Uncle Tete desperately. "So, one, two, three of us could not satisfy the lust in you. It must be a fiery one, an irrepressibly irresponsible lust. Well, you have made up your own bed very badly, so too, will you lie on it badly. I speak for all of us, we swear, we have no sympathy for you now. Rather, we have a basket full of contempt. Tete, I Osongo, am ashamed of you and of course they too," indicating her two mates, "are thoroughly ashamed of you. Mister General is right to do as he pleases and of course he is always right. You in fact are not only in a mess but in a more than double mess. You have shamed us and there is no question of forgiveness."

So said, the women walked away, disappointment and annoyance shouting all over them. The following morning, a major item on the news read: *"An alien swindler shown the red card."* The details then revealed who this swindler was – my dear Uncle. He was described as an economic saboteur of the worst order. The country's number one enemy; one who must leave within forty-eight hours. The news stunned all of us, including the drivers and domestic workers. Going to school was out of the question that morning. An alien breeze appeared to be insidiously breezing into the cosy compound. His business empire had suddenly been struck by an ominous storm.

Uncle kept within. He could not have the sympathy and love he badly needed at that time because his wives had equally fallen out with him. In fact, his household seemed to have been overpowered by the alien breeze. Through and through that day, the family vitality had turned into a strange debility. It was only the beginning. Each tick of the clock brought my uncle nearer to the deadline. By the following morning, he had only twenty-four hours left. I was anxious to see bulging suitcases but there was none. Curiosity however led me to the door of Uncle's room and I found it open. A peep into it did not indicate his whereabouts. I went round making everyone to understand that Uncle was not in his room. As they all became anxious like me, one of the gardeners rushed desperately to the front of the villa and announced that there was a body floating in the swimming pool. There was no doubt it was my uncle's body. At this point, things really turned sour, especially for me. The police was instantly informed and later in the day, it was no longer news that Mr. Tuka Tete, the flamboyant chairman of Tuka group of companies had rid himself of his own life. The reason for which was no longer news as well. I could not understand why uncle had to do that. It made me wonder about the rationale behind suicides which I questioned in the following quip:

> *If babies can endure the hard blows*
> *Of existence,*
> *Why should adults turn to suicide*

When their turn to endure comes?

Uncle was buried in the municipal council cemetery at Lushasha. The funeral was understandably low-key, and his corpse could not be taken to Katinda because of the circumstances of his death. Suicide is an abomination in the tradition of the Katinda people, so a corpse like Uncle's was untouchable. No one would have been prepared to receive it at the airport, had it been flown home.

A week after, there was a dramatic change in the family Uncle had left behind. The knot got loose and it became a question of each one for himself, and God for us all. The twelve other children easily identified with their respective mothers and then I saw the bitter truth dawning on me. I was the odd child that had made the odd number thirteen. Two weeks later – two gruesome weeks, I was on a plane back to my country, Katinda. The flight was smooth but I was very anxious. Anxious because I did not even know the country to which I was heading. I had left it as a baby so I had no memories about it. All the memories I had were being left behind me. I was, in fact, flying towards the unknown.

After the customs formalities at the airport, I was in no hurry to stop a taxi. Instead I took a walk around the airport, watching some of my co-passengers as they were being hugged on arrival by their loved ones who had come to welcome them. No one had come to welcome me, so I expected no hugs. I wandered out of the airport building and discovered that Yokin, the

44

capital city was scattered on different hills. The airport itself was on a plateau. I fed my eyes on the pleasant view and when I was satisfied I took out a letter which a maternal uncle had written to Uncle Tuka, inquiring about me. I had found it among his old letters after his death. I used the address on it to trace my maternal uncle. It read: Yankari quarters, Yoki city, Katinda. I knew I was going to get into a lot of problems trying to trace the house since there was no indication of the house number. I however decided to try my luck. I stopped a taxi, got into it and read out the address to the driver. He looked at me in a way I felt very embarrassed. I saw that his face was riddled with surprise and I was about to ask if there was anything wrong with the address I had read out. Shortly after, he ignited. The car lurched and after a series of coughs the engine came to life and we started descending. A few minutes later, he asked:

"Where you bi say yu di go?"

I did not quite understand what he was talking about, but from the words; 'where' and 'go', I made out that he was asking me to repeat my destination.

"I suppose I had earlier told you," I said doubting if I was making myself understood. "If I must repeat, I'm going to Yankari quarters."

"I beg nobi ting for vex," he pleaded. "Na for seka se pipul like yu, weh di waka long long waka, and na for eroplane, no kostom for stay fo that kayn ples."

I could not quite understand what he was talking about and so I just kept mute. When I

45

finally paid him off, I understood what he meant. I was standing in a place reeking with poverty, in fact a redolent of misery. Stench sailed irrepressibly in the atmosphere. The precarious houses seemingly leaned on one another indicating that they owed their existence on each other. If any misbehaved and gave way, then that would be the beginning of an avalanche. I needed to gather quite some courage in order to find out where my uncle lived in that quarter. When I found the courage, I asked, from a group of excited people, sipping a thick liquid which I learnt later to be corn beer. They were sitting on a long veranda of a decrepit hut. In reaction to my inquiry, one of them sprang up and asked:

"Which Massa, Kora?"

At this point, I realised that in order to survive, I had to understand the type of English that these people spoke to me – Pidgin English, I was told later. They seemed to understand me perfectly well but I had a lot of difficulties trying to understand them. I made a very special effort to understand them. I looked at the man who had just spoken to me and said half smiling:

"Kora Kekem,"

"Yu say Kora weti? Kora Kekem?" he still asked, in a bid to be sure.

"Yes, that's him," I said reassuringly.

"Oh yes. I knows him very well. Him is my neighbour. Goodman. Like each one of we. We all here na neighbour. And we all here good. Poor man must be good. If poor man no good then him worthiness na hell fire. My pikin make I finish this kpacha for my cup and I go take you for Kora Kekem house."

"Thank you sir, I'll be very glad."

When he had finished his drink he lifted my travelling bag and placed it right on his head. But before we started going, he asked.

"But yu bi who for massa Kora?"

"Me, I am his nephew, his sister's son," I replied.

"Where yu comot from," he asked.

"From Lushasha," I answered.

"Ah Lushasha. That go bi na far way place," he said.

"Yes, it's far," I said.

We both walked to my uncle's house, jumping over pools of water, animal and human waste. I could not resist the stench and so I had to take out a handkerchief which I placed over my nostrils. When we eventually got to the house, my benefactor knocked excitedly on the door, asking;

'Kwa kwa for yah"

There was no answer.

"Kwa! Kwa! Kwa! for yah, na who deh haus?" he shouted.

A faint voice answered and then a boy came over to open the door. It was a frail looking little boy. His legs looked like those of an ostrich. A lean craggy skin seemed to have been delicately wrapped on his skeleton. It was a wonder to me, the boy could move and talk at all.

"na you wan deh haus?" asked my guide.

"Yes, na mi wan," answered the boy.

"Y-y-e-s!" You nodi fear big man. Na so you di answer your papa? Na so your mami teach yu for answer big man? Come on, talk say yes sah!"

"Yes sah," the frightened boy answered instantly. His looks evidently evoked pity and suddenly, I felt like crying.

"Wu sai your papa go?"

'Yi don go work," answered the boy.

"Your mami nkor?"

"Yi don kari pikin go hospita."

"Al-right, this na wuna trenja eh. Be with am soteh your mami and papa come, you hear!" he said pulling his right ear.

"Yes."

"Shut up you nonentity! You say wetin again? N-y-e-s?"

The boy quickly recollected himself and then said, "yes sah."

My guide nodded approvingly and turned to me. "Yong man, na massa Kora Kekem haus be this. Dem no deh haus but na yi first pikin be this. You go stay wit am till him mami or papa come. I go still see you another time. My haus no far way from here, na only for that corna. By the way, my name na Man-Burden. Mi na papa for ten pikin dem. A born dem with two different woman. Yu go see all dem wen yu cam for ma haus. We go see small taym."

"Goodbye sir, thank you very much," I said.

"Thank you too," he said walking away.

I put my bag in the house, sat down and looked around me and started wondering whether human beings were actually the inhabitants of this house. I had to get used to, before I could convince myself that human beings survived such habitation. The house looked as rickety as any other in the Yankari quarters. Mice mingled around with impunity; they appeared to be bona fide members of the household. They constantly emerged from little holes at the base of the walls. The furniture comprised a long wooden bench and three chairs. There was no table. The floor was littered with crumps of food, here and there, a rusty spoon, a rusty knife and a number of repulsive objects. The walls were coated with soot and dirt like the other parts of the house. The house was always invaded by thick smoke each time cooking was going on in the kitchen. Never before had I witnessed such squalor. I used to see slums in films and documentaries but I had never believed that they were real. Now, I was living the experience.

The little boy was visibly scared of me and so went back into the room. I later learnt that he was ten but he looked less than six and his parents thought that he had not been ripe yet for school. I decided that I should stay outside and enjoy the freshness there. When I stepped out it did not appear much better as I was instantly greeted by the stench. I wondered if I was going to survive. At the side of the house was a gutter in which all kitchen waste from the houses that lined up along it was thrown. The waste was moistened by a constant pouring of dirty water into the gutter. This water was usually from laundry basins, from bathrooms, and from the kitchens. One unfortunate thing was the fact that the water was usually blocked by some thick slimy waste.

This was an apt agent of odious decay, producing the offensive stench that hung stubbornly in the atmosphere. It was not only a breeding but also a virile rendez-vous spot for mosquitoes and microbes. My whole alimentary system became oddly sensitive to the environment and I was overwhelmed by a nauseating feeling. This was my unavoidable fate, for I had no other place to turn to. I had to persevere and wait for my uncle, and moreover, it was quite obvious that Yankari was going to be my home for a good part of my life, if not the rest of it.

My uncle's wife eventually returned and inquired from the little boy whom I was.

Fortunately my uncle had talked to her about me and so she moved over to me to ensure that I was in fact the person she had heard about.

"My brother, wusai you comot your own?", she asked with interest.

'I'm from Kulashasha," I said hesitantly, having barely understood her.

"Na you bi my massa yi sista yim pikin?"

"Yes"

"Wus taym yu come?"

"Not quite two hours ago".

"Wustaym you leave that kontri?"

"About five hours ago."

"Yu mean say you comot there today?"

"Yes"

"Ee mean say that place no far way?"

"It's very far off. It takes thousands of kilometres to get there."

"Thousand kilometas, how come you use only five hour for reach here?"

"I travelled by air."

"By air, you fly like bird?"

"No, by plane!"

"By plane! Aeroplane kari you?"

"Sure of course."

"Humn," she murmured. "This wan go fit stay here wit we? Weh na for aeroplane yi de waka, yi clothes self na big big man pikin clothes; yi tok sef na for nose like whiteman. Alright you go wait for papa for haus yah," she concluded.

I nodded. She had earlier kept the child she had taken to the hospital on the bed in the room. So after the interview with me, she started her kitchen activity. My appearance and outlook had made her wonder if I could cope with life in Yankari even for a day. All things being equal, I was sure her conviction was not faulty but in a situation of no choice, one cannot help but cope with any situation, no matter its "uncopability." I could not have stood it for five minutes. I would obviously have left the environment with immediate effect for I would have surely had no business staying in such a place any longer than even a minute.

Later in the day, my uncle arrived. He had been met by Mr Man-Burden, the man who had guided me to the house. He promptly told him about my arrival. So that as soon as he entered, he embraced me fondly as if he had known me all his life. I was overwhelmed by his display of love and kinship. We then sat down to talk things over. After I had unfolded the events that had led to my unexpected arrival, he tried to comfort me. He assured me of protection. My mother was his younger sister whom he regretted had died in her prime. As he talked so touchingly about her, tears started darting out of his eyes. I found him a very sentimental man. I had no choice but to sympathise with the situation and inwardly pledged not to do anything to slight this poor humble man. My whole constitution in spite of itself, started adopting tolerance. I had to tolerate the nauseating environment.

As we were talking Mr. Man-Burden was heard calling out to me even before he had stepped into the threshold.

"Ah Kora Kekem! Yu de for haus?"

"Yes I de oh Massa Man-Burden."

"How for that we trenja na?"

"Na yi I di discuss wutam so."

"Good!" I just come back say, mek I salutam now for proper way. You know say trenja wey come far di bring goodluck for the first man wey him meet. Since na mi him meet first, then na my goodluck him dong bring. For that reason I don bring am kola."

He entered and sat down. He presented the kolanut he had brought to me. My uncle took it from me and broke it into lobes and gave me to share round. I was encouraged to also take a lobe and put in my mouth and began to chew like the others. It was the first time I had ever tasted kola nuts. Shortly after, Bakumeh, my uncle's wife, brought in a big bowl of cooked plantains and "koki" beans. The three of us sat round the dish which had been placed on the floor. I was eating "koki" beans for the first time and it was quite a palatable dish. Even if I had found it unpalatable, how else could I have filled the hollow that had been created in my stomach. It was time for me to discover many new things. A while ago it was kola nuts.

After the food, I told my uncle, I wanted to relax and I was given a mat which I spread on the hard floor and sprawled my tired frame on it. Uncle entered his room and brought out a pillow for me. The odour that came out of the pillow made me feel sick instantly but I tried not to throw up. I did not reject the pillow either. I had prepared my mind against slighting my uncle - the poor humble man. The pillow's softness nevertheless, provided me with the needed physical comfort. I therefore had to try all I could to suppress the nauseous discomfort. It was therefore not surprising that I slept off shortly after.

When I got up, I was sure I had slept for at least three hours. Daylight was already surrendering to darkness. I needed a bath very badly and when I mentioned it, I was shown the bathroom where a bucket of water stood in wait. I went into it tolerating the stench, which I was already getting used to anyway. But I wondered at the aggressive nature of the one in the bathroom. Then my eyes fell on a flat piece of plywood on the floor. When I kicked it, it was to expose a round hole, out of which very hot and visible air was emerging. Flies, fat flies, maggots, stout maggots hung busily around the hole. There were active cockroaches on the walls and the floor. I could not figure out what this meant. I learnt only afterwards that it was a pit latrine. But why combine a latrine with a bathroom? The answer at the time was beyond my imagination. Grudgingly, I covered the hole and in the same vein I had my bath using the only available soap – "coco soap." I could not wait to dry my body so I wrapped my towel round my waist and walked back to the house. I dried myself up and rubbed my skin with some left over skin cream I had brought from Kulashasha. After I got dressed up, Uncle Kora suggested that we went out for a walk.

As we strolled along my knowledge of poverty and squalor deepened. Yes, poverty here also meant squalor. The children I came by appeared craggy and ragged. And many others, especially the under tens, went stark naked exposing their vital parts to the hostile world of insects and germs. The skeletal structure of most of them was mirrored through their thin skins, with stomachs shooting out like inflated balloons, not from over feeding but from disease-kwashiorkor they call it. As we snaked through the twining paths between the crammed houses, a woman was sweating over a pot of meat on a wood-burning fire, some big drops from her fore-head actually augmented the soup in the large pot. She had in her hands a big stick which she used in stirring the fat slices of meat in the pot. Beside her was a pit latrine whose shed and flooring had collapsed. The churned waste inside the almost filled pit was actually an open sore to the naked eyes of all the passers-by.

It was therefore not unusual that the woman cooking the pot of meat could stand the sight and stench of the mess. She had already become so used to doing her business there that the in-hygienic conditions meant very little to her. Come to think of it, the meat which I was quite convinced was meant for dogs was actually being prepared for human stomachs. The house which stood by was an eating house which was regularly filled with customers. People were actually sitting in comfortably and eating without any qualms. The people as they ate, chatted excitedly and some were actually licking their fingers noisily, evident that the food was very appetising. I shook my head as I passed by and inwardly remarked that adaptation was the greatest of human virtues.

When darkness made its intrusion, we had walked quite a long way and then we entered a bar. A very crowded place with every soul inside sweating profusely. In spite of the sweat and odour, they smoked and danced as if they had to fulfil, at all cost, the appointment they had taken with dancing. I could have told my uncle I was not inclined to entering such places but I was not only helpless but haplessly imprisoned by my own decision to be complacent. I made sure I did not do or say anything that might displease my uncle and he was happy and satisfied. I was being entertained but he was barely spared disappointment by the grace of one of the limitations of man – inability to read the minds of others. I could do nothing but resign myself to the heat, stench, noise and sweat as I sipped down the bottle of coca cola, my uncle had bought for me.

We returned home quite late. I lay sprawled on a mat spread on the rough floor. I turned and looked at my little cousin who was lying peacefully on his own mat, close to me. His frame spelt out ill-health very clearly, yet he seemed to have no need for a doctor nor even medicines. I could not help but think of my recent past. The life back in Lushasha and then now, not quite a distance from a pig. I could not understand, nor would I ever understand such contrast. At one moment you are in Heaven and in the very next you are in Hell. Suddenly, my thoughts wandered further: for whom is heaven and hell created? Probably for everyone. For the past twelve years, I had been in heaven and now I have been projected to hell for a purpose I was yet to find out. But I could not understand one thing – my crime. What in the name of my ancestors had I done to warrant such a cataclysmic thrust into hell? Nor the thousands, in fact millions of men, women, babies and children condemned to this hell of a Yankari. In the midst of my turbulent thoughts, sleep descended like an eagle and winged me away.

When my eyes opened the following day, light was already prowling in through the rafters and the holes on the roof. I got up feeling tired rather than refreshed. I walked to the veranda in the vain hope of breathing some fresh air. I stood there for some time then I noticed my skin. I was stunned and I felt afraid, I might not survive it all. Then as I turned to return into the house, I saw my uncle's baby sitting smilingly on the laps of her mother. Her skin too had the same stumps-

stumps left by mosquito bites. Yet this baby sat smiling. I felt humbled and then I decided that like the baby, I would with fortitude and a smile take my fate as it came.

When the question of continuing my education came up, my uncle could not afford to pay my fees in a private secondary school, nor even get a place for me in a government secondary school. So I was enrolled in the final year of the primary school in Yankari quarters. Its only corollary with my former school was in the appellation 'school'. But then, I had resolved to smile at anything fate offered me. I worked with very little effort yet I always had the best scores. At the end of the year I came out top, in the final national examination, not only in my school but in the whole country. In this way, an opportunity was offered me in a reputable government secondary school, but I was a day student. I had to walk five kilometres from Yankari to my new school every morning. My uncle, his wife and neighbours were all very proud of me. I was the only boy in Yankari quarters to attend the reputable Central High School. Here the required text books and uniforms were given to students free of charge. Also, lunch was served in school for everybody including the day students. The requirements for admission were so stiff that only children with a very sound primary education succeeded in gaining admission into it. Unfortunately, children from the backyard quarters like Yankari hardly ever got such sound primary education, so it was not surprising that I was the only child from there to be admitted in the school. Even then, I did not owe my privilege to a higher intelligent quotient vis-à-vis the other children of Yankari, but to the good schooling I had had in the international school back in Lushasha. Most of my fellow classmates came from very good schools around the country or came from homes that could afford supplementary lessons for their wards. I did not quite relate with my fellow students as I seemed to be the odd child out.

I was the only student from a slum, and from some obscure primary school called Yankari School. I was the only boy who got to the school everyday sweating from a long walk. I was the only boy in the school who hardly talked about birthday parties, latest films, Sunday picnics, swimming expeditions and car ride at the weekends. Well, I had had such experiences but talking about them would seem as if I was day-dreaming.

I kept to my books, knowing that only they offered me the best opportunity to retrieve myself out of the slum conditions of Yankari. So it was no surprise that at the end of each year I got first prize of every subject. I did not think I was a genius, though many people thought so. The secret was just that my poor conditions had matured me faster than the rest of my classmates and so I had recognised what education could do for me earlier than most of them. Determination worked out my success better than anything else.

At the end of the seventh form, I did not disappoint the expectations of my well-wishers – the Yankari slum people. My name topped the list of students who had been offered government scholarships to study in the developed world. I chose to study medicine against the recommendations of the guidance counsellors. They recommended me for Engineering, having considered my top grades in Maths and Physics but deep inside me, I knew I wanted to quit the slum possibly for good and stand out as the hope of the living dead.

"Doctor Esong Tuka," the usher called out.

I heard my name only vaguely and I was not quite sure. The usher called out again:

"Doctor Esong Tuka"

This time I heard the name distinctly and stood up. I walked to the podium, with much humility, to take my oath.

4

No Armour Against Fate

It is evening and the last embers of the light of day are creeping out and disappearing into thin air. A look skywards, and the eyes will be sprightly welcomed by a wide expanse of blue, sky-blue. A few ticks away from the hour, the invisible hand on the invisible switch will switch off the warning light, and the sky and the earth will once again be plunged into darkness. The honest and the innocent that crawl and scratch the earth's surface will then start preparing to keep their various appointments with sleep, while the vile and the bane whose deeds must wait for darkness will bounce up like inflated balls ready for the feet of football crazy boys.

Sad Sam was one of the honest and innocent, so he faithfully kept his appointment with sleep on the rugged floor of his abode – a ramshackle kombi bus, which had been abandoned on the roadside for about half a decade. But for the occasional wailing of the bane mosquito, Sad Sam would always vow that there was not a soul on mother earth, whose nights could tally his own in depth, breadth and peace. This he always emphasised was because at the end of each day, he lay down with a clean, clear and open mind that dwelt on nothing but goodwill and the sleep that it so much desired. When the earth again reverently throws forward its hands to receive its light as dawn rubs its eyes to ascertain its wakefulness, Sad Sam equally gets up hale and hearty, ready for another laborious but rewarding twelve hours.

Sad Sam, sad about the refuse-dump almost swallowing up his residence and offering passers-by an eye-sore which had also given birth to an eternal stench that had continued to linger around that part of the city, decided to use his time and strength to get rid of it. Armed with a dilapidated container and a rickety rust-ridden shovel, both of which had previously been part of the dump, he carried heads and head loads of the rubbish to deposit in a far off valley. Yes, this was Sad Sam's avowed function which he hardly missed a day without performing. But the people, the people of Bakanda city never ceased to pile up more and more of this rubbish on the refuse-dump. As they did it, Sad Sam merely displayed an awkward sense of indifference. He went about his business behaving as if to say "forgive them, for they know not what they are doing." Nobody cared to appreciate his efforts, instead whenever he opened his mouth to tell them they ought not to do it, they gleefully called him madman.

There was this day, Sad Sam was busy filling his container, his shovel sinking deep into the refuse-dump and emptying into the container. Then the shovel struck a polythene bag bursting it open. The ensuing stench was rather repulsive and vomit inducing. Flies soon got the message and it was a matter of seconds before a swarm of them settled on the content of the bag. Sad Sam's curiosity was put aflame. He tore open the polythene bag completely and the whole content lay helplessly in front of him, attracting more and more flies. It was a well structured form having the size of a well fed six-weeks-old puppy. The softening limbs, head and trunk showed, it had been decaying for the past three days. Sad Sam turned it from side to side and noticed that it was not a puppy, the decaying thing had been part of humanity. In fact a baby. He sighed and then murmured, "damn it, it is all the madness of existence." He put his shovel aside and looked around and found four pieces of wood. He also found some nails. He rushed to his home and got a hammer. He put the pieces of wood together and made a coffin. He put the remains of the baby in it and closed it. Then he picked up the shovel and filled his container with refuse. He placed the coffin on the filled container and then lifted it onto his head. He stooped and picked up the shovel and walked towards the valley. When he put down his load, he started digging a hole. When he was satisfied, he took up the coffin carefully and placed it into the hole saying out of dust you came and back to dust you shall return. He stood silently for a minute and then filled the hole. He made a small cross on which he wrote the letters RIP, and placed it on the small mound that he had formed, muttering: "the least anything human should deserve is a burial." He emptied his container and walked back to the refuse heap.

While he was preparing for the next trip, Dan Anyang, a former classmate was passing by and saw him. He paused and ventured to attract his attention.

"Hello Sam" he called out.

Sam did not do as much as wink at his direction. Rather, he kept down his shovel, spread out his arms at an angle that could allow his hands to grip the container at both sides. He eased it up to his head and off he left for the valley. Dan Anyang then gave up and went away.

Later in the evening, when Sad Sam was about to close for the day, he came round again.

"Hello Sam," he called out.

"What is it now Anyang, what for goodness sake is your problem? Why don't you want to leave me alone?" Sad Sam retorted angrily.

Anyang was confused, he had thought that on the previous occasion, Sam had not recognised him, let alone remembered his name. However, he soon found words again and asked.

"So you can still remember my name, Sam?"

"Why can't I, or you too think like the rest of them that Sad Sam is mad, don't you? Don't worry folks, I'm yet to be mad, probably madder than madness."

"But Sam, could you spare me some time. I mean some of your time?"

"What for?"

"I wish to offer you a drink, if you don't mind?"

"Well, I don't mind, Sam said reluctantly after considering the matter for about fifty eight seconds. "Who am I" he continued, to say no to an offer from the blue. I think I'll be much obliged to you Dan. But do you mean it is right away?"

"Of course" said Anyang.

Seeing that it was after all time for him to stop work, Sad Sam put aside his tools and led Anyang to his home — the abandoned kombi bus. They went in and Anyang took a seat, while he took out a bottle of water, washed his hands, feet and face, drank some and then took a comb out of his pocket and combed his hair carefully. When he had finished, he indicated that he was ready. The two friends walked out leisurely to "country-man's bar." All eyes were fixed on them, as everybody expressed surprise at the fact that Sad Sam could stand the company of another human being. They had been used to seeing him alone. They found an empty table and sat down talking amicably to each other, which surprised the people, even further.

After the order for drinks had been given, the two friends conversed loudly, reminiscing about the old school days as their glasses of beer inched downwards. Each time they inched out completely they refilled them and continued the conversation. They talked endlessly about the London days, when both of them were pursuing different courses at the London School of Economics. Finally, after Dan Anyang had paid up the bill and they were ready to take off, Sad Sam tapped him on the shoulder and said, "Anyang I'm not ungrateful for your kind gesture. It's exactly four years since I sat down for a drink like we have just done. No soul thinks I am sane and none will venture to come close to me. Therefore I'm left alone, all by myself. In fact, alone in a human-hive. But I don't think I hate it, for I've grown to disregard them – my fellow human beings. Disregarding them appears to make me happier. I'm now master of myself, subjected to the whims and caprices of nobody. Not even yours, Dan Anyang. I accepted your offer not because you dictated to me but because my instincts did. And my instincts are mine, nobody else's. They hinted me that a man like you, like the rest of them would hardly cope with my present way of life. So you could not have meant any harm by inviting me for a drink. The whole of humanity, including you Anyang, call my way of life madness, hence they don't hesitate to keep off me as suddenly as they find out. There's no gainsaying about it, for in fact, there is hardly minimum compatibility between two people having opposed wavelengths. Mine is a peculiar wavelength Dan Anyang, peculiar because there are hardly two of my kind in a society and so everybody finds me objectionable and useless. However, I did not expect anything far from that, for any person that must be regarded by a society as useful must behave within the norms of that society. Be they acceptable or unacceptable norms. A thief my brother, is a very useful member of a society of thieves. Any deviant is nothing short of a madman. I think I'm a deviant Anyang and so it's obvious to everybody, Sad Sam is mad. Your person sitting there Dan, is merely tolerating me, probably because of our old relationship. You surely must be wondering, trying hard to figure out why I, Sad Sam, the dashing Casanova, has turned into drab misery. It has to be, Anyang, for brother, there's no armour against fate – the madness of existence.

Dan, some sage somewhere coined the saying; "one good turn deserves another." It is in this light that I wish to suggest that you come over here tomorrow at this same hour, so that together we have a drink on me.

Don't look surprised. I know my looks, my abode and my behaviour are considered abnormal but that should not be a bother. Just trust me and keep the appointment. I reckon you will not regret sparing some of your precious time to a madman. You know wisdom can sometimes come from madness. Remember our good friend Dapo who used to live at West end. The alcoholic Dapo who always exonerated his misdemeanour each time he was drunk with the lyrics of some lady musician's song:

"Much madness is devinest
Sense
To a discerning eye
Much sense the starkest
Madness."

Dan Anyang had just recently been transferred to Bakanda city. He works with an international organization and has until now been moving from one nation's capital to another. He now has the fortune or rather misfortune to work in his own country's capital. For all he knew, his friend Sad Sam, a humorist in his London days had returned home to set up a newspaper. He had decided to exploit his rich sense of humour by taking up a column in the paper and captioned it *"Reason with Sad Sam."* For some sinister

66

reason his paper was banned and himself jailed. Later, as the years rolled by, Dan Anyang got up one day, by then he was working in Managua, and heard a radio broadcast that made reference to Sad Sam as a gubernatorial candidate of the People's Progressive Party. He later won the elections and was Governor of Nugorno State. A few years later the survival of civil government and consequently democracy was jeopardized by military ambitions. When this happened Sad Sam had been blacked out. Dan Anyang was therefore totally taken aback to find him in his present circumstances. He had become worried and curious to know exactly what might have been responsible for his friend's present predicament. He wondered whether he was, as it was widely claimed, a madman. He was interested in finding out.

So at the appointed time, Dan Anyang promptly went over to "country man's bar." Surely too, Sad Sam was there on time and they both found seats, each on the opposite side of an empty table on the veranda of the bar building. The beer came and the two friends began to sip in silence. Minutes later, Sad Sam broke the silence.

"Anyang as I was saying before we separated yesterday, "much madness," to borrow a leaf from the wisdom of the lyrics of what Dapo used to sing, "is divinest sense," but that is to a very perceptive eye that cares and on the other hand what most people might regard as sense might be "the starkest madness."I suppose Dan Anyang, that rings a bell."

"Sure it does." Anyang said approvingly.

"You see brother, people consider it sensible to plunge into this imbrioglio called existence with the fury that only compares with recklessness. Rivalling with, plotting against, stabbing, clubbing and destroying one another for the craze of survival. What for, I may ask. What for brother?"

Anyang merely shook his head in wonder and pity without saying a word.

"What for Anyang?" Sad Sam insisted.

"For nothing" Dan Anyang replied in spite of himself.

"For nothing Dan?" Sam asked almost threateningly.

Sam burst out derisively with a long loud laugh that made the crowded bar stir, and stare at them.

"Well Anyang," Sam continued, "it is not for nothing. It is to satisfy the desire to be the only cock around that crows."

"If it is to satisfy that desire, then each man had better find himself an Island and live there all by himself," put in Anyang.

"Foul, that is foul reasoning Anyang. Man, I tell you brother, is a paradox. He wants to be the one and only cock that crows but never can survive all by himself. So an Island to himself and only himself, will give him the greatest dissatisfaction ever. What man wants, is to be the one and only cock that crows amongst millions and millions of other cocks, for his very nature is, a being-with-others. He gets the greatest satisfaction when he dines and wines extravagantly while others feed from dustbins.

Just watch the cocks that crow in this society – those to whom you and I look up to. He makes sure he squeezes those around him dry of even the blood that nature had endowed them with. Yet we all admire and clap for them each time there is the least opportunity. They are almost worshipped, in fact worshipped. You see now, the source of rivalry with, plotting against, stabbing, clubbing, garrotting and destruction of fellow human beings."

"I now see Sam, where what might make sense become stark madness." Dan Anyang said sorrowfully.

"Imagine my exploits in London" Sam continued, "my success as a journalist, my tenure of office as governor, all these to satisfy that drive to be the one-and-only cock that crowed and then in the final analysis I'm looked upon as a madman, an undesirable".

"Undesirable even by those who had benefited from you?" asked Dan.

"Look at that!" Sam exclaimed and burst into a long loud laugh, which simmered down to: "Dan Anyang, I tell you, there's no armour against fate."

"Sure there seem not to be," agreed Anyang.

"And talking about being a successful journalist, that was only ephemeral. My journalism became unpalatable to the one-and-only cocks that crowed at the time. Unpalatable because it made the people they trod on to know they were being trodden upon. And that was the truth. This truth threw me in jail ruining my career as a journalist. Nevertheless I am not ungrateful, for the same truth gave me the honoured seat of governor of Nugorno state and its attendant paraphernalia. You must be wondering how I ascended or rather descended from a governor's castle to living in an abandoned, battered-rickety-junkety Kombi bus. The same people who now sneer at me used to cheer whenever they saw me. I was their hero in politics by the grace of the truth I stood by as a journalist. They fanned me and I was up there, one of the ones-and only cocks that could crow. Then the barracks boys went loose and struck. Once more I found myself falling from grace to grim grass. Grim grass, I tell you Ayang because the jails those boys threw us into were only comparable to what the bible calls hell. The scolding, whipping, in fact the general torture, I was subjected to was as devilish as dehumanising. I turned into a weeping boy, me a weeping boy. The reason for the torture I knew not. Or was it because I had offered to rule a people that I should be so tortured? I could not understand. Before I was eventually taken for trial, I had spent thirteen maddening months in detention. I came out as lean as a rake, looking as tattered as a chicken just rescued from a pit latrine. The same people who had praised and applauded me when I was their governor sneered and jeered when they saw me caged in a security truck, being taken to court. At my trial, the court, though a kangaroo one set up by the ambitious boys from the barracks, found nothing incriminating against me. They discharged and acquitted me. The following day they duly released me from detention. This was the price of honesty and uprightness for which I pride myself on. My fellow colleagues, went in seriously. Some registered as many as two hundred years imprisonment—what a ridiculous sentence, I hope they will live as long as their terms. Anyang it was amazing I came out a freeman but it was not the same Sad Sam. Rather, it was a traumatized Sad Sam who came out free. My wife and children jubilantly took me home, but soon discovered I was rather odd. They rejected me quite easily. I was no longer their type of man. Every move I made embarrassed them. They could not cope with my newly acquired behaviour and so shortly after, I found myself in chains and enrolled in a psychiatry ward. They, my wife and children were visibly showing quite some concern for me and I say they genuinely wept and were worried about my state. After a while I was discharged but my family did not find me any better and so days later I was, in spite of myself, registered as member of a village mad house.

The psychiatrist claimed to have had his training from a great cult house in India. His treatment was very harsh full of incantations that made no sense to me. Quantities of concoctions were forced down my throat and I was subjected to untold humiliation – treated like a disfavoured animal, all because they had claimed I was mad. When I eventually had my way, I walked out on my doctor, damned my own home and my family and found residence in the solace of that abandoned Kombi bus, rickety and junkety as it is."

Anyang felt the pangs of the story penetrate his entire frame of mind and shortly after his eyes started watering. He took out his handkerchief and gave them a cleaning. Then he asked Sam if his children still attended to him.

"What for?" he snapped. "They have their own madness which is existence to cope with. Since they dropped the suitcase here, full of banknotes, nobody has bothered to pass by and see how I fared. However, they do not even need to, for their own preoccupations cannot submit to the bothers of a madman. I am a madman, they say but do I care?"

"Can I give you a helping hand," asked Dan.

"How?" Sam asked curiously.

"Get you out of this. Honestly, I want to do something for you." Dan said anxiously.

"Absolutely nothing. You can't do anything for me, Dan Anyang, as a matter of fact, fate and I have met at a crossroads and I have no armour against it neither have you Anyang. Besides, I feel rather exalted than spurned at this crossroads. For one thing, I think I'm of better use to the people."

"How?" Anyang asked surprised.

"I am committed to clearing the refuse dump that fouls the air in this part of Bakanda city. It is my avowed function – one of Bakanda city refuse collectors."

Dan Anyang looked at his friend wide-eyed and then took a deep breath.

5

Acquired Drinking Efficiency Syndrome

Tanko's lips were moving feverishly as he was making a desperate effort to sing "dombolo." He was on his way home, reeling on the road like a child learning how to walk. His entire body was odiously reeking of alcohol. An oncoming car almost knocked him down as he continued to 'zigzag' his way even on the highway. In an attempt to cross to another side, he had not bothered to take the necessary precautions, so the car surprised him just before he had finished crossing the last lane. Apparently the driver was quite attentive as he slammed on his breaks just on time. The car screeched to a halt, a few centimetres from Tanko. He remained on the spot transfixed by terror. Suddenly he took up his right index finger to his forehead saying: 'in the name of the father' and then to his chest and of the son and…'

The driver got out of the car, held him and treated him to two agonizing smacks on each of his flabby cheeks. Then he pushed him aside, clearing his way. He got back into his car, spat on Tanko saying, *'malheureux, il faut chercher ta malchance ailleurs'* and then he switched on the ignition and drove off. Instantly, hot urine started running down Tanko's laps, down to his feet, snaked onto the tarmac, ran down the road a while, and then into a culvert. This experience cleared off some of the alcohol in his bloodstream and the 'zigzagging' became slower almost going to a halt. At this point he was not only reeking of alcohol but also of the urine that had soaked his pants and pair of trousers.

The early morning home coming was on a Sunday. The cocks were just picking up the second phase of their crowing at dawn, when he was laboriously climbing a small hill off the main tarred road. On top of the hill stood the house in which he was a tenant of a single room. A pig was busy digging into a garbage heap that was only metres away from his house. It was grunting as it dug persistently. Tanko stood for a while and listened to the pig. Then he turned to it and said, 'stop grunting, you pig-of-a-bitch. All honest animals are peacefully asleep and you are here still digging and grunting, therefore disturbing the peace of dear old nature. Besides you pigs stink like the droppings of your spouses. I really wonder what people find in pork that it sells in our markets like hot koki. It even competes with drinking houses. "I pity them, eaters of pork," he said spitting at the grunting pig. As he spoke, the pig was busy minding its own business. He took it for an affront, so he stopped brusquely, stamped his feet on the ground and said, 'shi-she-e-aie.' The pig heard him and grudgingly grunted away.

Meanwhile Tanko had left his house at noon of the previous day, immediately after a hasty brunch of *'beignets et haricot.'* His destination was 'Mimbawi Bar,' a spot where people used to drink not only all day long but also all night long. This had been Tanko's routine ever since Saturdays had become work free days.

However, he had managed to arrive at his doorsteps. He fumbled into his pockets, for his bunch of keys. Fortunately it was there. He took it out but could not identify which key was what. He decided on one, but it could not get into the key-hole. He tried again and again but no luck so he decided to try another one but his hand had begun shivering like a drenched chick left in the cold. As a result he could not use any of the other keys. He resolved to hammer on the door with his thick boots, calling out to his twin sister who was living with him temporarily.

"Ebinko! Ebinko!" he called. Get up and open this damn wretch of a door for me."

She got up, rubbed her eyes and asked sleepily, whom it was that was knocking.

"It's me, me Tanko! Open this wretched door for me," Tanko shouted.

"I suppose you went along with your own key. What prevents you from using it?" Ebinko asked puzzled.

"Now Ebinko, you'll do as you're told ok." Tanko said imposingly. "And you'll do me the favour of not asking me too many questions. Now you'll open this door for me, won't you?"

"I want to be sure it's my brother before I open," said Ebinko.

"W-h-a-t Ebinko, do you mean you can't recognise my voice?" shouted Tanko again.

"Sure I can, but nothing stops a thief from imitating it."

"Well, well, well, Ebinko. It's your brother speaking, your twin brother. My full name's Tanko Tanhassanninku Tanko. I've got my keys but I'm afraid I can't get it into the key hole. I'm too drunk to be able to do it," Tanko said pleadingly.

Ebinko was convinced that it was her brother, and when she opened the door, he saw someone with all kinds of stains all over his clothes and his boots had been roughly polished by marshed-red-earth. He was literally stinking like one who had just come out fresh from a pigsty. He was in fact a sorry sight. She reluctantly gave him her hand and he immediately took it. As soon as he got in, he slumped on a chair looking as if the misery of the entire world had caught up with him. Nevertheless, the smell that accompanied his breath told the whole story. Ebinko tried hard to ignore him and went back to sleep but she could not. She decided to talk to him.

"Tanko, you could not think of coming back home ever since you left?"

"No, I couldn't," he managed to reply.

"Why?" she queried.

"I had my drinking to do," he said.

"Your drinking Tanko! Since when had drinking become your own. Your property?" she asked with much concern.

"It's not only my property but also an immunity I count on very much."

"An immu … what Tanko?"

"What you've just heard. Keep asking," he urged.

"Why shouldn't I ask, when you've always kept me worried by your endemic absence from home. How can a man have shelter but prefers to stay out in the rain. Since I came here, we've never sat down to discuss important matters affecting our family. You're always out and when you return it must be very late and you must be drunk. You left this house since yesterday afternoon and you've only just returned. Tanko, you ought to be ashamed of yourself. How come you are almost always making a nuisance of yourself. Every honest man enjoys the peace of sleep at night but you are only out to disturb this peace. If you had a mirror in front of you now, I'm sure you would not be able to hold back your own tears. You have made yourself a slave of alcohol's. What a shame Tanko."

"Thank you very much dear sister. All my life, no one has been able to oblige me with such a homily. I'm now prepared to switch from being a nuisance, if only I can help it. But unfortunately I can't because I'm suffering from the Acquired Drinking Efficiency Syndrome," concluded Tanko.

"What did you say, Tanko?"

"Exactly what you have just heard. I'm suffering from ADES!" Tanko said calmly.

Ebinko, felt so confused that she broke into sobbing and asked why the brother had not made any effort to report his problem to any doctor nor take it to the hospital. But drowsily Tanko ordered her to keep quiet, saying;

"Stop it, stop it. I've got no patience with foolish sentimentality. Whoever told you, the treatment for ADES is in hospitals? You imagine my frequent and long visits to 'Mimbawi' are for what?" asked Tanko.

"I suppose you're not kidding yourself Tanko. How can such a deadly disease be treated in a bar – drinking place?" said Ebinko really alarmed.

"Who in the name of peace, put it in your head that ADES is deadly. Have you seen or heard about any health organisation that is giving itself sleepless nights and headaches because of ADES? Or has anyone heard about international conferences and seminars on ADES? Please let's catch some sleep," urged Tanko.

"Catch some what! – Sleep?" she asked herself. "How can sleep even come around me after I have heard my brother's a victim of this deadly disease that everybody's talking about?"

She heard him as he began to snore. When she observed closely, she noticed that he was, in fact, deeply asleep. Ebinko could not wait for the day to break completely. She could not imagine how she would lose her brother at the prime age of twenty-five. She knew nobody had so far survived AIDS, yet her brother wanted to play it down. She hoped that it was simply the language of a drunkard. She had known him to be one who spent his time drinking alcohol, and getting drunk had made him a disaster but becoming one of the victims of AIDS would even make him an absolute disaster. "We came to the world together," she thought, "and now he has to leave me behind. How come we are so different?" He was such a bright boy at school while I was dull. He's tall slim and almost handsome whereas I'm short, stout and – according to many people – almost ugly. Anyway, he's and alcoholic while I'm a teetotaller and now he's got AIDS whereas I haven't. She kept wondering about the fate of her brother as the dawn was gradually setting in.

"How can an illness just come out of the blue like this and it is killing so many people," she wondered."Is it actually God's way of punishing reckless people like my twin brother? I really wonder, because I've known some very nice people who have been swept away by it. It is really a pity especially when we are told that there has been no cure, so far. It is generally believed that God can never place a load on a head that can't carry it. If that be the case, then the AIDS thing may likely be an invention of some reckless adventurers, who should own up and tell the world how it all started, so that a clear idea of how to solve the problem can be got. If on the other hand it is a sort of punishment from God, then there's hope that he would show us the way to handle it. Well, it has now hit me right in my own house. Tanko, my twin brother who's much talented in getting into touble, has again done it. I remember how he was almost dismissed from primary school because he had broken the nose of a fellow pupil. Our father had to intervene energetically to prevent his dimissal. He had to go through several secondary schools by the time he completed secondary education. He had always had someone to shoot his troubles for him. But this time, it'll be a trouble shooter of a kind."

As soon as the day's businesses began, Ebinko fished out three hundred francs from her handbag and put in her purse. She went to the water container and took a half full cup of water and washed her face and mouth. Then she took her dress off a hook on the wall and wore. Such a dress is commonly called "Kaba ngondo" a name adopted from the Douala language by the whole of the southern part of the country. The dress suits all occasions and women, especially the elderly, like it very much. Cultures that believe in the immediate replacement of a dead person find it most suitable for funeral wake-keeping occasions. She also selected a headscarf to cover her untidy hair. Before she stepped out, she threw a pitiful glance at the snoring Tanko.

On the main road, she stopped a taxi and announced, Nkolmassi. But the taxi driver just drove off without saying a word. She expected him to say, "I'm sorry, that's out of my way" or simply "sorry" before driving off. The rude behaviour always gave her the jitters. It only confirmed the impression she had had about the town, the first week she arrived there. The impression was that the people were hostile, especially to strangers who neither spoke nor understood their language. The market women never said thank you after one had bought from them. They could go as far as throwing insults at one if they offered prices, they thought were very low. She could not understand why inhabitants of a capital town like Nkolo should be so hostile. She always wondered how strangers from other countries felt if she, a stranger from one of the provinces of the country felt bad and insecure. She stopped the next taxi and the driver asked if she could pay fifty francs more than the normal fare. She considered the proposal for a few minutes and hopped in. She dropped on the main street of Nkolmassi and walked about one kilometre more into the *"quartier,"* and then crossed a dirty stream. Just after the stream was Ni Mfondu's house, which was her destination. Ni Mfondu was the head of the external elites of their tribe, resident in Nkolo. When she arrived the house, the doors were still securely locked. She tapped on the main door and waited. A few minutes later, it was opened and she was let in. She greeted and sat down. Then later, she asked if she could speak to Ni. One of his wives went and informed him. Promptly he came out, still in his pyjamas and asked if there was anything wrong.

"Ni" Ebinko began, "It is my brother ni."

"Is he dead or dying?" asked Ni Mfondu anxiously.

"Not exactly ni" she said timidly.

"Then what's the matter?" he asked getting more anxious.

"Ni, it is like this. He went out drinking and only returned this morning."

"So what happened?"

"He said he had had the deadly disease AIDS."

"AIDS?" asked Ni Mfondu surprised. "AIDS from drinking?"

"Yes Ni" answered Ebinko.

"That must be strange. Were we not told that it is got ... from ..eh well, where is he now?" asked Ni Mfondu looking embarrassed.

"At home Ni."

"Still at home. Ok, just give me a minute or two and I'll be ready."

Within ten minutes, Ni Mfondu was ready and he and Ebinko walked hurriedly to the main street where they took a taxi to Tanko's. They met him still sleeping and snoring on the chair. Ni examined him critically and turned to Ebinko saying; "he doesn't seem to me like someone suffering from AIDS, rather he's like one who had had too much to drink."

"He said it himself Ni. He said he was suffering from AIDS," Ebinko said defensively.

"Has he been tested for HIV infection recently?" Ni asked.

"I don't know Ni" Ebinko answered.

"Then we had better get him up and find out if he had," Ni suggested.

Ebinko shook her brother from sleep and he got up frowning and cursing. She indicated to him that he had a visitor. Then he rubbed his eyes several times and sat up. Finally, he realized who his visitor was. Then he hurriedly tried to put things in place but Ni Mfondu asked him to calm down. He sat back looking silly and ashamed.

"I'm sorry Ni" he started apologizing.

"You're sorry about what?" Ni Mfondu asked.

"Sorry for this mess Ni. The room is … eh … very untidy and eh... mm, I look rather unkempt" said Tanko apologetically.

"Well never mind. In times of crisis things get disorderly," said Ni reassuringly.

"Crisis, what crisis Ni?" Tanko asked feeling embarrassed.

"Do you want me to believe, there's no crisis?" Ni asked.

"Well the infamous economic crisis. That shouldn't make our homes disorderly Ni," he replied regaining his confidence.

"I don't mean that. You mean you don't have any health crisis Tanko?"

"Health crisis. What health crisis Ni? I don't understand." Tanko said getting worried.

Ni Mfondu turned and looked at Ebinko and Tanko too turned and looked at her. She felt rather uneasy as the two pairs of eyes were fixed on her. She looked at Tanko and said,

"But Tanko, when you returned this morning, what did you tell me?"

"What did I tell you?"

"Did you not tell me, you were suffering from eh the acquired immune deficiency syndrome – *AIDS*?"

"What! I did say that?" Tanko exclaimed., "you must be demented or you got that in a dream. How dare you ...", he shouted menacingly.

Ni Mfondu waved a hand at Tanko and he stopped.

"Well," said Ni Mfondu, "there must have been some misunderstanding. Now Tanko, when you came back home, did you discuss anything with your sister?"

"Nothing Ni, absolutely nothing. As soon as I returned, I opened the door and then sat on this chair and later fell asleep on it."

"That's not true Ni." argued Ebinko.

"You mean I'm lying? What the hell had I to discuss with you that I couldn't wait for the day to break?"

"We spoke to each other when you came in." She insisted.

"So what did I say?" Tanko asked infuriated.

"What I've told Ni, that you have *AIDS*?" Ebinko answered.

Tanko looked at his sister menacingly and wondered whether she was in the right frame of mind. Even if he had such a problem, she would not be the person he would confide in, so he did not quite know what to think. At this point Ebinko asked him:

"Tanko, do you remember who opened the door for you when you returned?"

"Me, remember? I had earlier said so. I opened the door myself, walked in and slept on this chair."

"Tanko, that's not true. You had problems putting your key into the key-hole and you called for my help. I then opened the door for you and then we started talking to each other." Ebinko said confidently.

"Give me some time to think Ni," Tanko requested.

"Well go ahead and think," Ni Mfondu consented.

After about fifty seconds, Tanko hit his forehead and said, "Now I can remember what I had told her. I had asked her to stop bothering me about my drinking habit because I had been struck by a disease called Acquired Drinking Efficiency Syndrome (ADES).

"Acquired Drinking Efficiency Syndrome. That must be a good one," Ni Mfondu said amused. Now, I understand the root of the problem," he continued, "well Tanko, your sister took your ADES for AIDS – Acquired Immune Deficiency Syndrome, and like the good sister she is, she had to show concern by running to me helter skelter in case I could be of help. Now that I'm here, I think we should find a solution to this your ... eh ... ADES thing. It might not be as deadly as AIDS but it is deadly all the same. So how did you get to acquiring it?" Ni Mfondu asked.

Tanko was taken aback by the question but he managed to find his voice: "Well Ni," he began, "I only started drinking when I had my present job. It was my first job ever and you know how hard it is to find jobs these days. So when friends came to congratulate me on my success, they ended up taking me out for a drink. They wouldn't want to hear me ask for an orange juice or anything soft. They insisted on my drinking beer and so I started drinking. Also at our elite meetings fines are in terms of crates of beer and I felt staying off it would be tantamount to losing something special in the business of living. Again among my present circle of friends, a man who doesn't drink alcoholic liquor is looked upon as a baby. And at my age, who would want to be regarded as a baby Ni?"

"Thank you Tanko. I asked you to tell me this not because I wanted to embarrass you but because I wanted to start tackling your illness from the source. I can tell you the main source of this drinking syndrome of yours is friends. And if I may ask, are these friends of yours bachelor boys like yourself?"

"Most of them are," answered Tanko.

"I won't ask you to stay away from your friends but tell them you've been banned from taking alcohol for one year, for medical reasons. And before the year expires, I'll contact your father and you'll have another excuse. Fortunately, there's an elite meeting next Saturday. I'll put forward the point you raised about the nature of fines, and at the same meeting, you'll swear by the gods of our ancestors that a touch of alcohol on your lips should make them descend on you with their clubs. I think I've done what I can, so I must go back to my own house now."

"I'm awfully sorry for the inconvenience Ni," said Tanko soberly.

"Not at all," responded Ni Mfondu as he prepared to step out of the room.

Ebinko who then felt as if a great weight had been lifted off her shoulders went to see off Ni Mfondu to the main road. Tanko slumped back on the chair and waited impatiently for her to return

6

Tears Are Not Forever

Akpata Ajongi lives in one of the houses crawling at the foot of Meyonga hill. His is easily the best house in the area. Its mud walls have a coating of cement from floor level to the rafters. The frontage, which forever seems to beckon on the hill, easily catches the eye of every person passing by. The attraction is the blue and white colours that adorn it. The house has a big yard. Big enough to allow for a deep well and space enough for children to play. The well makes up for the rampant water cuts by the Mboka Town Water Corporation. Mboka is a fast growing town and like most such towns, it is riddled with a lot of social problems. These problems sometimes put people under such pressure that family life becomes a nightmare. In the meantime, the last drizzles of the persistent July rain had just ceased on a Saturday evening and some cool air had taken over. It breezed down from the hill and intruded unobtrusively into the houses downhill. Akpata was briskly concentrating on the pages of a journal, when the pendulum of his old grandfather's clock struck seven times. He glanced at it and resumed his reading. He had just finished his dinner, when he transformed his dinning table into a reading one. His beautiful wife, Arrah, was playing with their children in another corner of the room.

"Arrah dear" Akpata called out pleadingly, "you and the kids are making much noise. It is disturbing my concentration."

"So what do you want us to do?" asked Arrah mockingly. "Stop playing and start mourning?" She pursued.

"Don't misunderstand me, Arrah. I just want you to be considerate. Now then, may I suggest that you take the children to the Abang's to watch television. Saturday programmes are usually fantastic."

"Aren't you ashamed to suggest something like that, A.A?" retorted Arrah.

"Ashamed Arrah, why should I be ashamed of making a simple suggestion," Akpata wondered aloud.

"Simple suggestion indeed. Why would I have to leave my own house to some other person's only because I must watch television? Are you waiting for heaven to come down before you buy a TV set for this home? And you complain about the noise made by your own children. You wish them dumb then? Akpata, I tell you it's over my dead body that my children will become dumb in order that their father might read journals. I'll encourage them to be as noisy as their late grandmother used to be. If what I am saying hurts you, go and rent a big apartment in which you would have a comfortable study, far removed from your madding wife and children."

"You have started being provocative but remember Arrah, there's time for everything." Akpata reminded her.

"Ne-e-y-i-sh tchaym for eve-ery-tch-ing. I have for ever heard that expression but I'm yet to be sure when that blessed time will come," Arrah said even more provocatively.

"Easy dear, easy. I don't need to remind you that God's time is the best," said Akpata clamly.

"E-e-e-z-t-e-e-z-y my gnash – nobi we go weit daso. How man yi pikin go du?"

At this point Akpata thought it better to remain quiet. He simply covered his face on the top of the table as if he was reflecting on what his wife had just said.

Although Arrah had been putting up a stiff opposition against going to the Abang's she had earlier in the day promised Mrs Abang that she would be at her's to watch that evening's episode of "Kabeyene." She really liked watching TV programmes but doing so on a screen that did not belong to her was rather disappointing – it took away some of the pleasure. She had persuaded her husband, in vain, to buy one. He had always complained about the lack of money. He could not afford the luxury of a TV set and still keep the family going for three months. Such explanations did not impress Arrah and she refused to understand. Later that evening, she wore pullovers on the children and carried Promise, the younger one on her left side just above her hips and held Hope, the elder one on the left arm and stepped out of the house heaving a protracted sigh that culminated in "A-a-a-a-h-a, man yi pikin go die suffa fo maret haus."

The concentration Akpata longed for in order to understand what he was reading disappeared as soon as his wife stepped out of the house. He could not waive with ease his wife's remarks, especially the last one before she left the house. He wondered at the conception that she was suffering in his house. He felt so bad about it that he put the journal he was reading aside, stood up and stretched out his almost two metre stature until he felt a sharp pain in his chest. When he stopped he also noticed that his joints were paining. This immediately reminded him of his age.

At thirty-two he felt, his body was losing its flexibility. He yawned loudly and went outside to embrace the darkness. He could not go further than his door steps and after pacing his veranda for a while he returned into the house. He sat on one of his cane chairs, leaned backwards and placed his feet on the centre table. His mind swept back to Arrah and he remembered the brightness that shone in her eyes when he proposed marriage to her. It was the second time he had proposed to a girl. The first time he did so was to a girl called Mgbati. Things were working out as planned but after a while the reverse was the case.

Mgbati had been his course mate at the University of Bujana. During the second semester of the first year, she could not resist the magnetic pull that brought her close to Akpata. His fleshy cheeks had a slight depression whenever he smiled and when he was excited his eyeballs shone with the brilliance of a cat's. He had a mustache which he meticulously kept trim and tidy. Girls were particularly pulled towards him because his manner was unrepelling. His composure and aura never carried the placard: "*keep off Mr. Handsome is approaching*!" Mgbati did not need a sliding tackle to fall for him when he picked on her. For over three years they had both been the "fufu and eru" of each other. In the M.A. year they made up their minds to get married. Mgbati took him to their home town to introduce him to her parents. When they got there, they found the whole family anxiously waiting to receive them. After the welcome ritual was over, Mgbati's parents insisted on speaking the local language. It did not take them anytime to realize that their potential son-in-law was a non-native. Without mincing words they immediately asked their daughter where he came from and she told them Mangwana.

"Mangwa… what?" they exclaimed with anger – where on earth is that? You have the guts to bring an alien to this house and tell us you want to marry him? *O-o-tio, lai lai* – not when we are still breathing this fresh air and drinking water."

They left the prospective husband and wife immediately and disappeared into their bedroom. The two lovers just stood looking at each other wondering whether the drama was real or unreal. It turned out to be the beginning of the end of their relationship. Mgbati had to succumb to loyalty to her parents. Months later, when Akpata was leaving Bujana for good, it was a disillusioned Mgbati who saw him off at the airport.

Back in Mangwana, he started another relationship when he was yet unemployed. Maria was the name of the girl. She was working in a local brewery and she took care of Akpata but it did not take her long to get tired of caring for an unemployed adult and so she easily brewed trouble and the relationship ended.

A year later he got a job in the Civil Service and was posted to Mboka. There he first met Arrah, a smooth ebony-coloured girl who stood a little above 1.7 metres. She was young and succulent like a hibiscus flower in full bloom. She bore the grace of a dove in her manners, walk and gait. She was only eighteen and Akpata twenty-eight. Two months after they had first met, they were married and eleven months later they had a son whom they named Hope. After Hope it took them only ten months again to have another child. Again, it was a boy whom they called Promise. Things had not been easy with the young family but Akpata had always maintained a very supportive posture.

As these events went through his mind, he rose from the cane chair and went back to the reading table but still he could not concentrate, so he switched on his radio-set to listen to the news at 8.00 p.m but the reception was very poor. He fished out a screwdriver and began to unscrew the knots that kept the components of the set together. It was not easy getting the radio repaired so he kept himself busy with the screws and knots. At ten O'clock Arrah returned, with the children who were already asleep. She took them to bed and they slept almost immediately. She returned to the living room and picked up a copy of the Mangwana Tribune and started reading an obituary. When she had finished reading all the obituaries in that copy, she put it down and picked up another one and still opened to the obituaries page. She wondered to herself why she enjoyed reading obituaries and in fact she usually opened newspaper pages for none other reason than to read them. Having read the last obituary she looked up and observed that her husband was still absorbed in what he was doing. She needed somebody to talk to and so she decided to interrupt him.

"Akpata dear, I suppose in the final analysis death is the best thing that can happen to man."

Akpata was very busy repairing his radio set and was paying no attention to what his wife was saying. She repeated her statement but again it fell on deaf ears. She touched him on the shoulder and said:

"Is it that when people are repairing radio sets they become temporarily deaf?"

"Eh! What's that supposed to mean?" asked Akpata.

"It means you had better give that 'mukong' radio to an electronic repairer if your repairing it, makes you deaf?"

"I still don't understand you," said Akpata absentmindedly.

"How can you? I have said one thing twice over and it could not as much as prickle those your rabbit-like ears."

"Those my rabbit-like what?"

"Ears!" Arrah exclaimed provocatively.

"Now Arrah! You don't kid your husband like that. Watch your tongue. If you let it too loose, it can exacerbate the anger in a fiery temper. Can you calmly tell me what you were trying to say?"

"I was saying that in the final analysis, death was the best thing that could happen to man."

"The best think how Arrah? You mean when somebody you love dies, it is the best thing that has happened to you?"

"No, not that. I am referring to the victim. If man dies, then that is the best thing that ever happens to him. In other words, death is the best thing that ever happens to the dead."

Akapa stopped his radio repairing completely and faced his wife squarely.

"You mean ... eh... you mean Arrah, that you prefer death to life?"

"Precisely so," Arrah answered with much enthusiasm.

"Can you tell me why?" Akpata asked with interest.

"Life is inexplicably harsh Akpata. It's like the eternal hell fire that burns to punish people charged with evil deeds. But on the other hand, death as far as I know is peaceful. As peaceful as sleep devoid of all dreams; no examinations to worry about, in fact no moments to excite. You do

94

realise that deep breaths engender peace and therefore the final breath should engender even greater peace."

"I see Arrah, but why don't you do as much as pinch it off?"

"Pinch what off Akpata?"

"That cumbersome, harsh 'bobo' called life."

"But it's not easy. I've had the misfortune of having been given it and it is hard for me to get rid of it, all by myself. I am like a bud that has grown into a perfect branch, something else has to cut me off from the main tree."

"There you are Arrah. Something else has to pinch life off you since you lack the courage to do it yourself. You could not prevent it being offered to you and since getting rid of it, you must rely on someone or something else, you are doomed to live until your benefactor puts a stop to it."

"True, I am doomed to live until whoever gave it to me takes it back. This is the more reason why it will be a great joy for me if the hour comes."

"But before that hour comes you think that life has nothing to offer?"

"It might have much to offer but not to people like me. As a child I was flattered by the cushion of riches that had been offered me by my parents. I enjoyed quite a comfortable cushion but it slipped beneath me and my tender buttocks hit hard on the hard floor of want. My father's life had been whisked off to the unknown and off he had gone with all that had been hope and good

95

life for me. Life took up a new phase and presented me with a path full of foolery, thorns, faeces and people like you."

"Me too Arrah?" Akpata asked, looking embarrassed.

"Is it something to ask? If I avoid stepping on a thorn it is obvious I must step on faeces. You know how hard it was before I got through secondary school. And then you came by and I married you thinking that my own share of hardship was over. A civil servant with not just a degree but two must obviously be a man of tremendous potential and a flaming future. But months have gone by, years too have and our existence is a drab-hand-to-mouth one. We still live in an apartment whose toilet facilities are shared by man and pig alike. Our tired 'footroen' is all we can afford for a car. Our children are condemned to attend the over crowded public schools with run-down facilities. I am condemned to listening to blurred music from a defective radio set whose main problem is old age and let me tell you, Akpata, the best I will do one day, would be to break it on the floor piece by piece. I just cannot cope with it all. When will my own earthly salvation come?"

"It had come and gone," Akpata said teasingly.

"It came when?" Arrah asked.

"When you were a child. You mentioned it just now."

"But is that enough? Why must I be embroiled in luxury as a child only for it to fritter away just when I begin to understand what it means to be rich?"

"You must count yourself lucky. Other children were, as babies, only rescued from dustbins and pit latrines and they have grown up, still not knowing what comfort is like. Arrah, suffering is a passing phase in life and quite necessary too. It is only very just and fair that you go through it. This is the reason why things have been going wrong, especially with me."

"Going wrong, going wrong, things have been going wrong can't you right them? Can't you get rich like other civil servants? What do they have that you don't have? Many degrees and diplomas for nothing. Can't you get yourself promoted to a position where you too can get chunks of the national cake? Can't you go on missions like others and return to swell your pockets with allowances? Look at you, you had applied for a government house ages ago and you are not even a millimetre nearer to getting one. Even loans that others get to buy flashy cars you are not able to get. I am sometimes worried if I am married to a man, a real man." She said feeling really bitter and frustrated.

"Woman, I just wish to beg that you hold your tongue," Akpata said calmly. "Don't drive me to a nerve-breaking crisis. Is it getting rich that is your mission on earth? Have you befriended death because your husband is not rich? Note my dear, I've been in the civil service for only a little over four years. Lots of other people have been there before me. If I don't get promoted, know that the position I would have moved to is occupied by another man who obviously had joined the civil service earlier than me. If I don't go out on missions then there is no mission worth going on. If other people go on mission just for the money then I am not one of such. By the way, I am a civil servant not a missionary. If I can't get a government house in which we can taste comfortable living, know that the documents are still being considered at the appropriate quarters. If I am not rich, know that as a civil servant I consider probity, a priority in the service of my country. If you think that the present state is bad enough, it will be advisable to turn round and look behind. You see our neighbours in the quarter who live ten in a single room and also people like the university student whose room gets flooded with excrement from the pit latrines each time it rains. On each occasion, she gracefully cleans up the mess and puts things in order again and life continues. Put yourself in that student's shoes and you might not really mind our present state. Arrah dear, try not to make me run faster than my own shadow. I have spent so much time studying, I was lucky to have found a job after three frustrating years in "chomeurcam." There's an awful line of dependants behind me but I need not be in a hurry. If I have to be rich, it will be an entirely different phase of life. That phase may come or not but I think keeping one's life jealously is what is important" Akpata said conclusively.

"I don't believe it is important, Akpata," Arrah said stubbornly.

"Are you sure it isn't Arrah?"

"Quite sure. To keep a poverty-stricken-life is sinful," Arrah insisted

"Do you love me Arrah?" Akpata asked softly.

"Yes, I do. Why?"

"And our children, do you love them?"

"Yes I do."

"Sure?"

"Sure, but why are you asking me all this," Arrah asked almost angrily.

"Then why do you prefer the luxury of death to your husband and children?" Akpata asked.

"I prefer it because it saves me from the exigencies of love, worries about the unknown and above all the scare of poverty."

"Then I will with no reservation say that you love neither me nor the children. Love should normally transcend everything including death. Death is surely a consolation as you believe, but for the aged who have fulfilled several missions on earth and exhausted their virility. Death is a consolation for old trees that can no longer shade the undergrowth but it is not a consolation for a young tree that enlivens the forest with bright flowers that lure the beauty of the bird kingdom. It is not for the young tree that provides the monkey with gyms. Death is not a consolation for a young woman whose breasts still flow with milk and has a duty to feed the world. It is not for a young woman who has strength enough to handle a hoe and feed mankind. Death is not a consolation for you Arrah who have a responsibility to me your husband and our children. If you tell me the truth that you love me and the children, then you must hold on to life tenaciously, no matter how harsh it might present itself. I wonder if you don't admire the tenacity with which swarms of afflicted people; lepers, cripples, the blind, deaf, dumb, the homeless and even the mad, hold on to life. All of them, like everybody else love to live while hoping that someday, somehow better days will come. Arrah dear, you might have taken marriage for granted and so married me in the hope that I will make your life comfortable. In as much as it is my wish to make you comfortable, I cannot go beyond my normal pace. We have been blessed with two kids already, so make up your mind and love us for the sake of love, forgetting the things that matter only to the flesh. Such love will make you realise the need for life even if it be a red-hot flame. Remember that it is for the love of you, the children, my ailing mother and my other relatives that I endure all the hardship I've been through and still am going through. Nevertheless Arrah dear, I hope one day, somehow, things will get better; for tears cannot be forever shed. It might be useful that you take note of these lines:

> On the subject of life
> Every journey to reflection
> Only leads to nothingness
> Therefore, for the good of life,
> Let's get some *somethingness*
> Out of much nothingness.

As Akpata went on talking, he realised that Arrah had lost concentration. He stopped, rubbed his hands and asked Arrah if she had been following up what he had been saying.

"Leave me alone ja-re," she retorted and remained seated.

Quietly Akpata resumed what he was doing, switching on the receiver from time to time to find out if his efforts had yielded any fruits. Each time, he found out they had been negative. As the night was growing older he packed up and then got Arrah up. She had fallen asleep on the chair. She stood up sluggishly and went into the bedroom. As Akpata was about switching off the lights, a heavy downpour ensued, the drops drummed furiously on the roof, providing a regular rhythm that tossed husband and wife off to sleep.

The following morning was blessed with much sunshine and incidentally it was a Sunday. Arrah had got up to prepare breakfast. When she had finished placing every item on the table, she asked Akpata to get up and wash his mouth. She cleaned up the children and soon after the family was at breakfast. As the food was inching away, Arrah asked if Akpata had succeeded in repairing the radio set.

"No" he answered and then asked to know why.

"I wanted to follow up Sunday morning Church service on the radio," Arrah said.

"That must be interesting," Akpata commented.

Arrah merely smiled looking at him.

"O.K." he asked, "I'll take up the repairs again as soon as we are through with breakfast." Akpata promised.

Immediately the table had been cleared, Akpata got his screwdriver and resumed the repair work. Promise was at his side watching with intent. Hope was in the kitchen keeping Arrah company as she washed up the dishes and pots, after about twenty minutes, Akpata fixed in the plug of the receiver into a socket and switched it on. The reception was quite good. He tuned from one station to another and found the results satisfactory. He called for Arrah and told her about his successful exploit.

"You can now listen to your Sunday morning church service," he said with a sense of fulfilment.

"That's great of you Akpata, you are a very ingenious person," Arrah said encouragingly.

"Thank you for the compliment Arrah. We seem to understand each other now. I wish that you can always trust and count on me."

"Don't I Akpata?" Arrah asked.

"Not always Arrah. Sometimes you give me cause to regret that I married you."

"Well you only have to understand that I am what I am. Only a woman."

"I do of course," Akpata said reassuringly.

As he spoke he tuned to a station, out of which blared the lyrics of a song

"O come and mourn with me awhile…"

"Oh! So it's Easter?" asked Arrah in utter amazement. "Akpata so it's Easter and we did not even know; see how pagan you and I have become."

"Pagan? I think that is a misnomer. I think the right expression is non-conventional Christians or better still non-church goers. Don't you remember that we both have baptism cards tucked somewhere in my trunk. Well, I don't go to church but I try to take care of my spiritual needs," Akpata said proudly.

"Good for you Akpata. What about us? Me and the children, how do we take care of our own spiritual needs?"

'In that case," said Akpata, "we'll all start going to church as from next Sunday.

Monday is usually a day of intense activity in Mboka. It's a day on which all roads lead to Okola, the business area of Mboka town. Akpata had left his house at 7.00 a.m. to take a bus to his office – the Civil Service Commission. His wife was at home doing the morning chores. Suddenly she observed that the house was very quiet. The kids were still asleep. She switched on the radio receiver and studio four was playing some good music. At eight o'clock a call for attention was made by the announcer; then she read the news flash: "The multi-storey building, housing the Civil Service Commission in Mboka, has collapsed and the casualty figure is already as high as a hundred. Medical personnel are hereby informed to rush to the scene and give assistance to the victims."

"My God," Arrah exclaimed and then without thinking shot out of the house like a discharged bullet. Within thirty minutes she was at the scene of the incident. Actually, the building had not collapsed but some of it's walls had cracked due to some slight sinking. The foundation had sunk about one metre deep causing a slight tremor which had sent people trembling. In an attempt to escape some people had jumped down from the sixth, fifth and fourth floors. Arrah was utterly restive as her eyes searched everywhere for her husband. She could not believe her eyes when they sighted him about ten metres away, helping to put an injured person into an ambulance.

She breathed out thankfully and waited for him to notice her. When he walked up to her she asked, "Akpata how did you do it?"

"Do what?" asked Akpata.

"Get out of the building unhurt,"

"Well, you know I always try not to lose my head in situations like this. I simply kept my calm and then walked downstairs after the hue and cry had died down. Many of my colleagues have died this morning simply because they had panicked when it all started. It pays to be composed you know. And by the way, what are you doing here?"

"What am I doing here?" Is that a question to ask me, A. A.? You expected me to fold my arms and sit comfortably at home on hearing that the building in which you work had collapsed?"

"I understand but what about the kids?"

"I left them still sleeping."

"You had better hurry back. They may get frightened when they get up and don't find anyone at home."

Akpata slipped a five hundred francs piece in his wife's right palm and then turned his attention to the injured. She walked a short distance away from the scene and hailed a taxi-cab to take her home. When Arrah stepped out of the cab she was faced with another worrisome crowd. This time right in front of her own house. A sharp current ran through her and she no longer felt herself normal. As she went closer, she found her son Hope crying hopelessly and pointing to the well. "Mama, mama, Promise has gone in there and has not come out ever since."

Arrah needed no further explanation. She headed straight for the well and attempted to plunge in. She was held down by the people who were struggling to take out her son's corpse. She could only wail, wriggle her body and wrench her free hand. They finally succeeded in taking out the body; it was stiff dead. Arrah saw her son and could hardly believe whether it was real or just an illusion. She let herself loose and went to feel her son's body. When she had done it she ran again to the well but was again held down. She could only wail and wail: "I beg let me go; let me go where Promise has gone; let me go and meet my child." After some time someone suggested that she should be left alone. When they let go of her, she rushed to the well, looked into it's depth and kept everybody who was expecting her to jump into it in suspense. She could not but gaze blankly as if in deep meditation. Later, she turned around and went to meet her son's corpse. At this point, neighbours surrounded her and started consoling her. Somebody was sent to inform her husband.

When Akpata came he wept like a baby, hungry for its mother's milk. Incidentally, almost a third of the population of Mboka was mourning. Many a family had lost a parent, a brother, sister, cousin or friend from the office building disaster. Little Hope was confused, seeing everybody around him weeping and his younger brother lying lifeless.

At six p.m. the following day, a procession accompanied the young corpse to its eternal resting place. When the coffin was lowered into the grave, Akpata in his farewell words to his son said: Promise dear it's a shame you've not been able to live and fulfil the promise you had for your daddy and mummy. You've slipped off our hands like a dream but we know you are not a dream. We know your name is boldly written in the register of humanity. All we have for you as a wish is that your young soul should enjoy peace profound."

Slowly he dropped in the first soil that was to bury his young son forever. Shovels went to work and Akpata and Arrah looked at each other, their eyes filled with tears. They turned and saw other crowds at other gravesides – burying their dead in the same way as they were doing. When the procession was homeward bound, Arrah took Akpata's left arm to give him vital support, which he needed very badly. As they got nearer their home, she whispered into his left ear. "Inside there, there's still Hope to take care of and I can remember, Akpata dear, *tears are not forever.*"